THE CONDUIT

THE GRYPHON SERIES
BOOK 1

WRITTEN BY STACEY ROURKE

FOR ELLIE AND MADDIE.
MAY YOU BOTH GROW TO BE THE HEROES
OF YOUR OWN STORY.
I LOVE YOU.

PROLOGUE

At certain moments in life reflection is mandatory. I found being squeezed in the scaly claw of a three story dragon to be one of them. As he shook me like an uncooperative toy, my rattled brain wondered how life had led me here. Could I have done anything differently to maybe *not* die horribly at the hands of Mr. Big-Green-and-Ugly?

But as my constricted lungs burned and ached for even a whisper of a breath, I knew there was no way I could've avoided this. No matter where I went. No matter what I did. They would've found me. It was inevitable.

A searing pain in my side signaled that my recently mended rib had cracked again. I opened my mouth to scream but could manage no sound. My head wobbled so hard it felt like it might snap off my neck. Black spots danced before my eyes. With them came flashes from a life that wasn't mine.

With tentative steps the girl walks through the smoldering, charred remains of her tiny village. Her bare feet are burned and blackened, but she doesn't waver. She lays a delicate hand on the shoulder of the half-eagle/half-lion creature that saved them all. Well...most of them. Some of the blood spilled in this emerald Ireland valley had been fatal.

His rants turned into nothing more than a ringing in my ears. One by one, my senses gave up. They retreated into the dark abyss and waited for me to join them there.

A look of steely determination overcame the girl's dainty features. "You didn't let us stand alone, and I will not let you."

The Gryphon snapped his beak and shook his enormous head. "No. This war will rage on long after your mortal life has ended. I have foreseen it."

"Then my heirs shall take up the cause as well!" She lifted her soot-covered nightgown enough to allow herself the movement needed to go down on one knee. Her glorious, ivory wings stretched out wide behind her as she pressed her fist over her heart. "It is my pledge to you that the O'Garren family will join you in this crusade. My people will be your warriors until we find victory or death."

The pain lessened. Peace replaced it. That pledge, made centuries ago, is what led me here. If the break-ins hadn't happened. If I had stayed in Michigan. I'd still find myself here, losing my grip on whatever tied my spirit to this world. Of course, now I knew that those break-ins were them looking for me. And they followed me to Gainesboro. As the last of my strength and energy drained from my body, the thought of my new home made me smile.

Gainesboro, Tennessee. That's where it all happened. That's where I learned the truth. That's where everything changed. That's where my destiny found me. And now, it's where I would die.

CHAPTER 1

Long shadows stretched out on the ground as the sun began to set behind the mountains. The competing snores of my brother and sister provided a soundtrack for the drive. I exited the highway and then took Gore Avenue right into the bustling burg that is Gainesboro with its staggering population of 849 residents. Seriously. The hub of the city took up less than a mile and looked like a scene from a Norman Rockwell painting. Red brick buildings lined the street, each decorated with their own colorful awning of choice. Large chain stores hadn't found this little corner of the world yet. The store owners here manned their own registers and called every customer by name. The most charming aspect of the town was the library. A bright, sunshine-yellow stucco, it stood three stories tall with elaborate, white moldings that had been carved with painstaking detail. Situated on top was a beautiful, Victorian-style clock tower. The ornate building might have looked odd in this minute town if not for the scenery that encompassed it. Gainesboro is nestled in the Appalachian Mountains, completely surrounded by their splendor. And now it would be our home. After a series of break-ins in our otherwise family-friendly neighborhood in Sterling Heights, my Mom made the decision to send me, my twenty-year-old brother, Gabe, and my fifteen-year-old sister, Kendall, to live here with our paternal grandmother. Mom would join us in Hicksville, USA, just as soon as our house sold.

I turned on Grams' street and smiled. She had on every light in the house, as if we could miss our target destination. Every year she had a fresh coat of paint applied to her story-and-a-half house to keep it a vibrant robin's egg blue. Frequent paintings kept the gingerbread trim and front porch a brilliant white. Since we were little, the upstairs of her house "belonged" to Gabe, Kendall, and me. On our visits, Keni and I shared the room that overlooked the front yard, while Gabe got the back bedroom all to himself. Just last year, Grams relented to our nagging and retired our cartoon character bedding for more grown-up prints. Next on our list was convincing her to get rid of the Snoopy shower curtain in the upstairs bathroom.

After I gave Gabe a quick shove to wake him, I climbed out of the truck and inhaled the rich mountain air. Hints of pine and wild flowers mingled in the breeze. It smelled like relaxation.

Gabe rubbed his hands over his face and buzzed head to chase the sleep away and then reached over the seat to shake Keni awake. She fell asleep with her face mashed against the side window. As her heavy lids struggled open, she attempted to untangle her long dancer's legs from the back seat before her brain had awakened enough for such a task.

"What? We...here?"

"Yep," I answered as I stretched my arms out wide.

The front door squeaked open as Grams bounded onto the porch. From the neck up, she looked like a typical grandma, her short, wavy, grey hair even worn in the standard old lady 'do. However, instead of a floral print apron or high-waisted pants, our

Grams had on a zebra print muumuu she customized to fall just above her knees and a pair of hot-pink wedge heels. We stopped cringing at her choice of attire years ago. Everything about her reflected her feistiness, and we adored her for it. In addition to the crazy way she dressed, she lived for fun, and always spoke her mind—often to our chagrin. She, like me, measured in at just over five feet tall and only broke the hundred pound mark by a pound or two.

"There you are! There you are!" she shouted. "Celeste, pull that truck into the garage. We'll unload it in the morning. Gabe, Kendall, get your fannies in here and kiss your Grams."

They both happily obliged.

Relieved to have the twelve-hour drive behind me, I took a few minutes to appreciate the beautiful surroundings. Quaint, impeccably-maintained houses lined the street and created a wonderful, small-town ambiance. I meandered to the garage and reached for the handle. Before I could give it a yank, a light appeared in my peripheral vision. I swiveled around to investigate. Above the neighbor's oak tree flew a glowing ball of light. The unidentified orb couldn't be a shooting star; it was too low to the ground. But it resembled one. I thought it was a small asteroid about to crash to earth — until it darted from one side to the other. Whatever this thing, it appeared to be alive. In an elaborate motion, it swooped down and buzzed past my head. I squeaked and covered my head with my arms. What the heck was this thing? I'd heard bugs in the South were big, but this was the size of a house cat! It swerved in again, this time close enough to brush against my hair. That garnered a squeal as I lurched to the ground in the fetal position. It whizzed past my head one final time. Then silence. Of course my brother had to pick that moment to appear.

"Whatcha doin'?" he asked. I actually heard the smirk in his voice.

"Big mutant lightning bug!" I yelled.

"Your courageous display must have scared it off, 'cause I don't see anything," he snickered. "But if you're worried it's going to come back for another vicious attack, I could pull the truck in. You can go hide inside."

With my arms still shielding my head, I tossed him the keys and rushed inside.

"Whoa! Where's the fire?" Grams asked as I flew in the door.

"Tennessee bugs are terrifying!" Safely inside, I relaxed and gave my beloved grandma a long awaited squeeze. "Hi, Grams."

"Hi, baby. Don't worry about the bugs here. They might be big as a Volkswagen, but they squish just the same. Now, come grab a plate. I ordered pizza."

Grams' heels clicked against the hardwood floors as I followed her to the living room. The pizza box waited for us on her glass-top coffee table. As soon as Gabe came back in, the three of us kids swarmed the tasty treat. We didn't bother with the plates but gathered around the box to eat. Mom would never have let us get away with that. Grams just hung back, a safe distance from the feeding frenzy.

"Want a slice, Grams?" I asked between bites.

"No thanks, I already ate."

"More for us," Gabe muttered through a mouthful.

We were well on our way to consuming our individual body weights in the cheesy goodness when Grams rose from her leather recliner. The determined look in her eye should've been our first clue something was up, but she lured us into a false sense of security with food. Wiley minx.

"While you're busy stuffing your faces and therefore can't argue, let's go over some ground rules for while you're here."

Our chewing slowed. Rules? At Grandma's house? What kind of backward, twisted dimension had we slipped into?

"First, I am not your maid. As long as you are here, you will pick up after yourselves. Are we clear on that?"

Kendall didn't hesitate. Her waist-length pony-tail bobbed as she nodded her agreement with enthusiasm.

Gabe snorted. "Yeah. Sure, Grams."

I swatted at my big brother. Then gave him a pointed look as I stated, "It won't be a problem, Grams." I got an eyeroll from him in response.

"Good. Secondly, you need to know your Grams has a life. Like tonight, I had to skip my Salsa dancing class so I could be here when you arrived." She wiggled her hips to demonstrate.

I quickly dropped my gaze to the table and tried not to visualize Grams Salsa dancing. Beside me, Gabe gagged on his pizza. The image must have crept in. Poor guy.

"That means I won't be here to entertain you. I expect each of you to keep yourselves busy and out of trouble."

"You don't have to worry about me," Keni declared, her ocean-blue eyes wide and eager like a happy, little puppy. She flipped her annoyingly perfect, golden hair over her shoulder. "I already looked online and found out when auditions for the Community Players production of *Cat on a Hot Tin Roof* are. I would, like, die for the chance to play Maggie the Cat!"

"Good girl, Kendall." Grams gushed and my sister beamed. Kendall wasn't trying to be a suck-up. It came naturally. Grams' gaze turned disapproving as she focused on Gabe. "What about you, young man? Your mother tells me that you have made no plans to go back to college after your little incident last year."

I paused mid-chew. Grams just touched on a taboo topic. One that could make Gabe transform from playful jokester to snorting buffalo in an instant. He had been on a full-ride football scholarship at Michigan State University when our Dad died in an accident a year and a half ago. A few months later, he decided to cope with his mourning by indulging in a little underage drinking. The result was a DUI, the loss of his driver's license, plus getting kicked out of school. His dreams destroyed, he moved back home. Since then if anyone even inquired about his future plans, he'd snap and a tirade would ensue.

So when Grams mentioned "the unmentionable," I braced for yet another blow up. To my surprise, he just gave a noncommittal "Not yet."

"Do you plan to get a job?" Grams pressed.

"Don't know." Gabe shrugged but didn't look up from his pizza. I couldn't tell if the tension in the room had actually reached a palpable level or if I was anxious it was about to.

Grams pursed her lips, clearly not happy with how this conversation was progressing. "How did you occupy your time back in Michigan?"

"Sports and stuff."

"I see. And did you become a professional athlete with one of those million dollar contracts?"

"No," he said with a sarcastic half-grin.

"Hmmmm. Guess you should probably get a job then, huh?" She raised her eyebrows, daring him to argue. Wisely, he did not.

"Probably," he answered.

"I could talk to Will Burke for you." Grams grabbed some napkins off the end table and passed them out. "He's the athletic director at Gainesboro High. He might be able to find a coaching position for you."

A spark of genuine interest lit up Gabe's broad face. "That'd be great, Grams. I'd really like that."

I marveled at this turn around. Maybe I wasn't the only one that needed a fresh start in a new place.

"As for you." Grams turned to me with narrow, pondering eyes. Her hands rested on her hips. "I know you have all the grace of a two-legged race horse, so what the heck do you do for fun?"

Ahh, nothing like the loving banter of family. Just gives me warm fuzzy feelings.

I pushed a strand of uncooperative brown hair behind my ear. "Until I head off to Rhodes in the fall, my plan is to sketch, veg, and basically give my pre-collegiate brain one last chance to be mush before it's forced to study and actually learn stuff."

Relaxation of any kind had been foreign in my life for a while now. After Dad died, I put my college plans on hold and concentrated on taking care of my family. Mom needed all the help she could get, so it hadn't really been a choice. With time, things calmed down enough for Mom to begin prodding me to put the focus back on my education and my goal of becoming an art teacher. First, I wanted to have a nice, relaxing summer. Then rejoin the land of the living as a freshman at Rhodes College in Memphis. I couldn't wait. Eighteen seemed a good age for my life to finally begin.

Pleased with how our "orientation speech" had gone, Grams plopped back down in her recliner. "Sounds good to me. You should head up to the clearing. You'll find plenty to sketch up there."

I wiped my face with my napkin to remove the remnants of the pizza slices I'd killed. "The clearing?"

Grams kicked up her foot rest and grabbed a gossip magazine off the end table. "Grandpa and I used to take you kids there when you were little, remember? Just outside of town, there's that walking trail that leads into the mountains. You follow it up and you'll find a clearing right next to a little brook. It really is lovely. I don't know why I don't go up there more often. Ooh, another celebrity baby bump watch! I love those."

Gabe quirked his eyebrow in Grams' direction and laughed. There was no question as to why Grams didn't hike anymore. Grandpa was the outdoorsman, not her. When he passed, so did her hiking days. But I did remember our trips into the mountains and all the amazing things we saw. It would be the perfect place to find inspiration for my drawings.

"That's a great idea, Grams," I admitted. "I'll definitely check it out."

Grams set the magazine in her lap and folded her well-manicured hands over it. Her eyes crinkled with a warm smile as her gaze shifted from Kendall, to Gabe, and finally to me.

9

"Kids, I think this is gonna be a pretty unforgettable summer."

CHAPTER 2

We spent the following morning unloading the truck and settling in. That lasted until early afternoon when Grams' "stories" came on. Then we were kicked out of the house and told to go find our own fun. Gabe and Kendall set off with their own agendas. My plan had been to check out the trail and stretch my artistic muscles—until I saw the mess that my darling brother left me.

While Grams' house was always neat and tidy, the garage held the truth of her pack rat tendencies. I hadn't realized how tightly Gabe wedged the front of my truck in amidst the clutter until I attempted to back it out. The wheels of my S-10 moved back an inch and a landslide of knick knacks, boxes, and outdated furniture pelted down on my tiny truck.

Fan-freakin'-tastic.

I climbed out, shuffled my way through the mess, then stood back to survey the damage, turning my head to look at it from all angles.

"What on earth happened?" Grams exclaimed as she rushed out of the house. "Oh! Celeste! What the heck did you do?"

"Just thought I'd rearrange the garage by ramming my truck into stuff," I grumbled.

Grams grimaced. "How bad is the damage?"

"I won't know until I unbury it. But from the way that armoire is leaning, I'm guessing there's going to be a nice dent in the side panel."

"Let me go DVR my stories, and I'll give you a hand."

"No, that's okay. Go back to your show. I caused the destruction; I can clean it up," I said and gave myself a mental forehead smack.

If Gabe was home, I would've made him help. This was his fault. But he'd gone up to the high school to look into an assistant football coaching position Grams found out about. I would go it alone.

Another exasperated groan and I got started. I cleared a path to the armoire, righted it, and checked out the damage. Not too bad, just one dent where the corner of it impacted. I could live with that. I noticed a chunk of wood sticking out from under my tire and squatted down to investigate. A chair must've fallen in the avalanche and I backed over it. Shrapnel from the chair carnage impaled my tire. It was hissing its way flat. *That* I couldn't live with.

Grams came back out toting an icy glass of lemonade. I snatched it, muttered a quick "Thanks," and downed it in one gulp.

"Ouch, that's a bad dent." Grams watched my face to gauge my reaction.

"It's not that bad. By any chance, do you know how to change a tire?" I motioned toward the flat.

"No, sorry. It's always been my feeling that the ability to change a tire is one of the reasons we keep men around." She gave me a strained smile, trying to make light of a bad situation.

"Gabe does, but it won't matter right now. I don't have a spare." I knew for a while I needed to get one but had failed to do so. It wasn't an issue until this very moment.

"That's not a problem," Grams explained. "It's a short walk to Hank's place."

"Hank?"

"He's the only mechanic in town. He'll loan you a spare. Gabe can throw it on. Then you can drive up to Hank's, and he'll get you all fixed up." I pondered how I would get the spare home but quickly dismissed it. Small town like this, Hank probably did pick-ups and deliveries. I guess some good came from everybody knowing everyone.

"Sounds good." I handed Grams back the glass and got back to work. I picked up a box that's contents were scattered across my hood, and I glanced inside. "Whoa. Who's this nasty-looking guy?"

"What's that, dear?"

I set the box down and pulled out the item in question. Carved from one solid piece of wood was a creature I had never seen before. Its head and wings were that of a bird, but it had the body of a predatory cat. It stood assertive and proud—chest out, feet planted wide. Its head was thrown back as if in a roar.

"Hmmm ... where did that come from?" Grams scooted up beside me to get a better look.

"You've never seen it before?"

"No, never. It must be an heirloom of Grandpa's. I know what it is though. It's the Gryphon. He's supposed to be half eagle and half lion."

I turned the sculpture over in my hands. Along the bottom, words were etched. "Protector of the Divine," I read. "What does that mean?"

"The legend was that the Gryphon protected divine items from those with evil intent."

"Divine items like what?"

"The Holy Grail ... Noah's actual ark ... I've even heard a couple of these guys guard the gates of heaven."

"So, he's like a big, mythical guard dog?"

Grams chuckled. "Well, look at him. Who would want to mess with that?"

"Good point." I flipped the mysterious sculpture over as I continued to examine it. Something inside of it clicked, followed by a faint whir. Before I could pull my hand away, a toothpick-sized wooden spike jutted out and pricked my finger. "Ow! Crap!" My blood dripped onto the sculpture, and I put my finger in my mouth to clean it off.

"Why the heck would anyone booby trap a wooden figurine?" Grams took the carving from me and set it down so she could inspect my injury. "Are you okay? Does it hurt?"

It didn't hurt. Odd as it seemed, a liquidly warmth had spread through my hand. "I'm fine. It surprised me more than anything." A succession of clicks, like a crank being turned, and the spike retracted itself. "It must be important to someone if they felt the need to protect it like that."

Grams scoffed, "It's so important it's been sitting in my garage for God only knows how long."

For reasons I couldn't explain, I asked, "Can I have it?"

Grams' penciled-in eyebrows shot up. "You want the booby-trapped artwork?"

Wordlessly, I nodded. I thought it best to refrain from telling her that as soon as my blood touched the sculpture, I felt a powerful draw to it. Or that the tingling heat from the spike's impact had spread all the way up my arm.

Grams scooped up the sculpture and dropped it in my hands. "If you want it, it's yours."

Those simple words filled me with a sense of joy I couldn't explain. Claiming the enigmatic item as my own felt right, and I had no idea why.

CHAPTER 3

I was wrong. Absolutely nothing good comes from being in a town this size.

As it turned out, Hank didn't offer a drop-off/ pick-up service. They loaned you the tire and sent you on your merry way—a fact that would've been helpful to know *before* I walked there. I was left to my own devices to figure out how to get the stupid tire home.

After failed attempts at alternative methods, I accepted my only choice and rolled the tire down Gore Avenue toward Grams'. Had it been a full-sized tire, things may have been easier. I could've walked normally and rolled it along. The stance I contorted myself into to push the spare tire along knocked me down about a thousand cool points, even if I was the only one who cared. My face blushed bright red as I squatted down and rolled it hand-over-hand.

Hank's entire crew watched me out the window, not even bothering to hide their laughter. Could even one of them offer me a ride home? No way! Turns out chivalry isn't dead, it's just busy laughing and pointing.

I trudged along for about half a mile before I stopped to stretch my back in front of the modest, independently-owned grocery store. I casually scanned the parking lot as I twisted and stretched my cramping muscles. That's when I saw it. Dread punched its way into my gut and settled there like a lead weight. A news van was parked in front of the grocery store.

No, no, no, no, NO! I am not going to be on the news rolling this infuriatingly tiny tire down the street!

Freshly motivated, I pushed that tire for all I was worth, rolling it as fast as I could across what suddenly seemed to be an endless parking lot. An inkling of hope started to build. I was about halfway across and hadn't been noticed. But then life intervened as it so enjoys doing.

From behind me, I heard, "Excuse me, miss?"

No! He's not talking to me. Keep rolling!

"Miss?" Whoever it was, he was following me.

I don't care if it's that old guy who hands out the million dollar checks. I'm not stopping. It's too mortifying.

"Whoa, hold on a sec." An arm shot out and grasped my elbow. I lost control of the tire, and it took off on its own. I watched in horror as it meandered down the sidewalk, across the shoulder, and out into the road. An oncoming car slammed on the brakes and swerved to avoid it. I hung my head and hurried to retrieve my tire. As I bent to pick it up, I mouthed an 'I'm sorry' to the irate driver. The gesture he gave in response made it clear my apology went unaccepted.

I heaved the tire against my chest and penguin-walked back to the sidewalk. Of course the guy waiting there had to be hot, because what kind of mortifying fun would it be for the universe if it was a sixty-year-old grandpa?

"I am so sorry," he stated, struggling not to laugh.

"No problem. I was hoping I would get to play in traffic at some point today." My tone was bitter enough to taint the joke.

"I was just going to ask if you needed help. But once you got that thing moving at Mach 10, I figured you were just gonna jump on and take off." The stranger's voice was thick with the amusement he failed to hide.

"I didn't even think to try that. It may've been easier." I laughed, grateful to see some humor in this.

He held his hand out to me. "I'm Alec Jeffries with Channel 4 News."

"Really?" The shocked word slipped out before I could stop it. If I had any embarrassment left in me, I may have blushed. Thankfully, I was maxed out. "I'm sorry. That was rude. You just don't look like a reporter."

Reporters on television always looked neat and professional. Alec didn't. His long, strawberry-blond hair was pulled back in a tight pony-tail at the nape of his neck. The shirt and tie he wore obviously weren't his. His tall, lanky frame swam in the oversized clothing. The tie was loosely knotted around his neck, the shirt untucked. Clearly he went for the comfort angle, not style—a fashion sense I could relate to.

He smiled at me in a relaxed, carefree way that added to his boyish charm. "I'm not. I'm actually a cameraman, forced in front of the lens against my will."

"How'd they rope you in?"

"The station I work for is out of Nashville, but I was born and raised here. When they heard about the cat story, they decided to send the local boy out. Much to his dismay."

"What cat story?"

"Haven't you heard?" He pushed his cuffed sleeves further up his arms. His crystal blue eyes sparkled with delight. "There have been panther sightings in the mountains."

"Panthers?" I repeated, not sure I'd heard right. "Did one escape from a zoo?"

He shook his head. "No zoos have reported missing animals."

"Panthers aren't indigenous to this area. Isn't it more likely to be a mountain lion or something like that?"

"That's what I thought, too." He shrugged. "Seems a heck of a lot more plausible. But there have been eye witnesses that swear it's a black panther."

I couldn't help but shiver. The idea of coming face-to-face with a carnivorous predator like that creeped me out. My reaction didn't go unnoticed.

"Don't worry. It hasn't eaten anyone...yet." Alec smiled mischievously. "So, are you going to tell me who you are, or do I have to guess?"

"Oh, sorry! I'm Celeste Garrett." I wiped my hand on my jean shorts before extending it to Alec.

"A relative of Gladys Garrett?"

"She's my grandmother."

"She was the school nurse, right?" Alec glanced down and realized he still had a hold of my hand. A pink glow filled his cheeks as he released it.

"Yep." I tried my best to suppress the grin that tugged at the corners of my mouth. "She's retired now."

"I remember her. She's a really nice lady."

"I think so."

Awkward silence. Then, "You never answered me. Would you like some help getting your tire home? Or are you just gonna get it going again and see if you can fly there?"

"As much fun as that sounds, I would love a ride home."

We were tossing the tire into the back of the news van when Alec commented offhandedly, "By the way, I got some great footage of you and your tire."

Damn it.

As soon as we pulled into Grams' driveway, I climbed out of the van and slid the side door open to retrieve my tire.

"You sure you don't want me to change that for you?" Alec asked for the third time.

"No, but thanks. You've already done more than enough."

The front door squeaked as Gabe stepped out onto the porch.

Alec didn't miss his entrance. "Your boyfriend looks ticked."

"That's my brother, Gabe. He always looks like that." I set the tire on the ground and slammed the slider shut. "Thanks again for the ride."

"I guess I'll see you around." Alec's face expressed a mix of hesitancy and hope. We suffered through yet another awkward silence before he gave a brief wave and drove away.

Tire in tow, I shuffled my way to the garage where Gabe intercepted me. "Did you just get dropped off in a news van?" His lips were taut as he fought back a grin.

I felt straightforward was the best approach. "Yes. I was rolling the tire home, and he offered to give me a lift."

"Wait, what was that?"

"What was what?"

"You were rolling the tire home?" Gabe's face turned red with the strain of his contained laughter. "How far did you get?"

"The grocery store," I muttered.

He exploded in hysterical fits. This was one of those moments when I wished I was an only child. I glared at him and waited for him to calm himself or choke on his own tongue. Whichever came first. I wasn't picky.

"You done?" I snapped.

"For now," he said, wiping tears from his face. "Although I'm pretty sure I'll have the same reaction when I tell people. And trust me, I will tell people."

"I'm not deluded enough to think you would keep it to yourself. I will give you my blessing to shout it from the rooftops as long as you do me one small favor first," I bargained, pointing toward the tire.

Gabe groaned. "Fine, I'll change your tire. But only if you help and let me teach you how to do it yourself."

"What if I help by handing you whatever tools you need but make no false promises to pay attention or absorb any information?"

Gabe rolled his eyes. "Whatever."

My tire-rolling escapade had eaten a huge chunk of daylight. The approaching twilight made it mandatory for us to turn on the outside lights to help illuminate our project. When Gabe determined that wasn't adequate, I became the official flashlight holder. I leaned against the door frame and tuned out as he worked. Midway through the project, Kendall came sauntering up the driveway. Tagging along behind her was a scrawny, baby-faced boy. His sandy brown hair was combed straight forward and hung into his eyes—a fact that seemed to bother him. He kept nervously pushing it to the side or flipping his head. And they say girls are the only ones who will suffer for fashion.

"Hi, guys!" Keni bubbled. "This is Keith. He lives across the street."

"Hi, Keith." I smiled.

From his crouched position, Gabe grumbled, "One day roaming around and she already found someone to follow her like a puppy dog."

I kicked his leg.

"Ow!"

"I met Keith at the library. He is so sweet!" Kendall gushed. Keith blushed at the compliment and flipped his hair again. "He read through scenes of *Cat on a Hot Tin Roof* with me. And guess what? I talked him into auditioning for the role of Brick!"

Keith's face blanched at that declaration. He may not want to audition, but more importantly, he didn't want to disappoint the pretty girl. Of course Kendall was clueless.

"You know, Keni." I tried to play diplomat. "Not everyone is as comfortable on stage as you are. Keith might be happier doing something behind the scenes."

Kendall looked at me like I spouted gibberish. "But he wants to audition. Don't you, Keith?" She unleashed the full power of her big, blue doe eyes on him. Poor, twitchy fella didn't stand a chance.

Keith's hair flipping reached a spastic pace. I started to worry he was going to inflict bodily harm on himself. "Yeah...uh, sure....it will be, uh...fun."

"See?" Kendall said, beaming at her victory. "We're going to head inside and rehearse a few more scenes." With that, she took Keith's hand and led him into the house.

"Not for too long!" I called after her. "Grams will be heading to bed soon."

"Okay!" she chirped.

I watched as they walked through the door. "Do you think she realizes the effect she has on boys?"

Gabe paused in removing a lug nut and looked in their direction. "I think she's completely oblivious. Just like he is that it isn't a compliment when a girl you have a crush on wants you to audition for the role of '*Brick*.'"

"Why's that?"

"Sub-context of the play—unanswered questions about Brick's sexuality," he explained with a shrug of his meaty shoulder.

"Oh, definitely not a compliment if your female crush asks you to play that part," I agreed. "How the heck do you know that?"

"American Literature class at MSU."

"You mean the one semester you took?"

"Wanna change your own tire?"

"Nope."

"Then drop it."

"Fair enough."

He went back to work, vigorously struggling to loosen an uncooperative lug nut. Boredom set in and my mind began to wander. I'd like to say that I was debating philosophical issues that plagued mankind, but that's nowhere near true. The crickets chirped, the leaves danced gently in the breeze, and I checked out mentally. One leaf broke free from its stem and flitted down past a glittery, yellow beak. That got my attention. I peered closer. Perched among the branches sat the most regal bird I had ever seen. It looked like an eagle, but the colors were too bright, too vibrant. The head and neck of the mighty bird were the color of spun gold, its body the hue of freshly polished bronze. The noble-looking creature cocked its head and examined me.

I pushed myself off the door frame and stepped closer. The creature seemed to have a mutual interest in me. It turned its head side to side like it was trying to figure me out. I was so focused on the animal that I didn't hear Gabe calling me.

"Cee, I need the light. Cee? Hello? Celeste!"

"Oh, sorry." I stumbled back over and readjusted the light.

When I glanced back at the tree, the bird was still there. Something about it had changed, though. It seemed to be glowing. I looked around for an outside source of light. There was nothing. I blinked rapidly to clear my eyes. That didn't help. The light grew brighter. A soft, white shimmer emanated from the eagle.

I wanted to get Gabe's attention so he could witness this. Unfortunately, I couldn't find my voice. The illuminated eagle rose from its perch and hovered just above the tree. The flapping of its wings was slow and methodical, like treading water. The glow became brighter, the equivalent of a street light. It was like a beacon in the sky that only I could see. I toyed with the idea that I could be hallucinating.

In one dramatic gesture, the mighty bird swooped mere feet over my head. I stumbled backward, lost my footing, and fell against my truck. It shot off in the direction of the mountains and left behind a trail like that from a sparkler. The trail pointed straight to the mountain range.

With the bird gone, I regained the ability to speak. "Did ... you ... see ... that?" I stammered, scrambling to my feet.

"What? You falling into the truck? That's not really a new thing for you," Gabe muttered as he pulled the jack out from under the truck.

"Look!" I exclaimed, pointing at the sky.

He casually looked up. "A shooting star. Cool."

"It wasn't a star! It was a bird! It glowed!"

Gabe shot me a questioning look. "What'd you do, doze off while you were standing there?"

"No! I'm telling you it was a glowing bird, and it was right there."

With one quizzical eyebrow raised, Gabe snorted. "I'm sure it was. Hey, remind me to ask Mom if she hung out near power lines when she was pregnant with you."

"I know how this sounds, but I'm telling you the truth."

"Whatever you say. If there was something there, it's gone now." He wiped his hands on an old cloth from the garage as he walked inside.

I stood alone in the darkness, watching the trail fade away. I couldn't shake the feeling that there was a message behind it. A sneaking suspicion told me that message was "Follow me."

CHAPTER 4

My tires crunched across the gravel as I pulled into the parking area at the base of the mountain trail. The sun blazed high in the sky on this gorgeous eighty degree day, with just a faint whisper of a breeze. I climbed out of my truck and flung my satchel of art supplies over my shoulder. This trip into the mountains held two purposes. The primary reason was to stretch my artistic muscles by sketching some magnificent Tennessee landscape. The secondary reason I wasn't comfortable in admitting, even to myself. I secretly hoped to get another peek at that mysterious golden eagle.

I stepped on to the path and felt as though I'd entered another world. One minute I was in the wide open space of the parking area, the next completely encapsulated by the beauty of the mountains. Sunlight filtered through the towering trees to cast a hazy, enchanted glow on the scenery. I breathed in the peace and serenity the mountains offered.

A short hike later and the soft, bubbling of a brook told me I had reached my destination. I ducked under a low-hanging branch, and my breath caught. It was loveliness defined. There was a break in the trees which allowed beams of light to shine down on the tiny creek like a spotlight. It gurgled rhythmically as the water coursed over its rocky base. Next to the brook, a large tree had fallen. Wild flowers, moss, and leaves decorated their fallen comrade in a beautifully messy arrangement. I wandered over to it and sat down, then closed my eyes for a moment and tilted my face up to let the sun warm my skin. I inhaled the smells of the forest. Floral and pine intermingled. Every color in the rainbow was represented in the collection of wildflowers that peppered the soil. It seemed that the trees, in their massive size, had taken a step back to give their tiny friends a place to prosper.

The desire to capture this breathtaking beauty invigorated me. I pulled out my pad and pencils and immersed myself in drawing after drawing. For hours I drew and sketched. Time escaped me. I lost myself in the shadows and details on the paper. When I stopped to stretch my cramping back, I was shocked to discover it was already dusk. Not wanting to be in the woods alone after dark, I bent down to collect my things. Something moved to the right of me. I wasn't alone.

Perched not twenty feet from me on a nearby branch was the eagle. A chill ran through me. Birds as a rule aren't scary. Unless they can light up, in which case uneasiness is justified if not expected.

I ignored the hair standing up on the back of my neck, swallowed my own trepidation, and called to it. "Hey, pretty birdie."

The eagle responded to my acknowledgment by lifting off its branch and landing on the fallen tree an arm's distance from me. Up close it was bigger than I expected, a fact that made me bite back a squeal.

"Aren't you bold." I noticed a slight tremble in my laugh.

Careful not to spook the avian creature with talons that can tear flesh from bone, I moved at a pace that would make a snail look speedy as I reached into my bag for the sandwich I had brought. I broke off a piece of crust and laid it on my palm. As I extended my arm to the eagle I struggled to control my nervous shaking. A gasp escaped me as it snatched the bread with its sharply hooked beak.

Its lack of hesitation made me wonder if it was a lost pet. The majestic colors would make sense if it was a rare, expensive bird. Maybe it wasn't my most brilliant idea, but I decided to test this theory by attempting to touch it. With a trembling hand, I reached out to the mighty bird. It held perfectly still as the tips of my fingers made contact with its silky feathers.

A sudden, blinding flash exploded around me. My head began to pound. I brought my hands up to massage my now throbbing temples. The eagle hopped closer to me. I looked up in surprise as it touched my arm with its beak. Another blinding flash overcame me, this time accompanied by a fun hallucination. As I looked in the bird's eyes, I could've sworn they elongated—the pupils expanded. Its eyes became … human.

I scrambled off the tree trunk, head swimming, vision blurring. A wave of nausea slammed into me, no doubt a combination of my intense headache and panic. I spun toward the bird, afraid to turn my back on it.

"What are you?" I screamed, my voice bordering on hysteria.

The eagle lowered its golden head and pulled in its wings. A soft glow began in the torso of the bird. In seconds the glow spread through its entire body.

"Oh, no." I gasped. "Not again. Look, you seem like a nice enough … mystical … thing. But you have to stop the glowing and brain flashes. I'll…I'll help you find your owner, who's probably used to this stuff. But you have to stop doing … that. Okay?"

The bird paused as if to consider my rant, then shook its head. My mind reeled yet again.

It understood me.

The glow intensified. I shook my head and backed away from the bird as if denial could stop this from happening.

Before me, the luminescent creature began to grow. Its light reached a blinding level. I shielded my eyes but tried to peek around my arm. Its expanding size no longer resembled a bird. I couldn't tell what it was anymore. I felt I should run, but the mixture of morbid curiosity and fear rooted my feet to that spot.

Like a switch had been flipped, the light vanished. The eagle was gone. In its place was a woman—of sorts. Her face was flawless beauty, made odd by the golden feathers that cascaded from her head in place of hair. Her curvaceous body was absent of clothing but adorned with bronze feathers. Gigantic wings of the same color sprouted from her back and fanned out behind her.

That was my brain's limit. My fight-or-flight mechanism kicked in, opting to run. I tripped over my own feet and landed flat on my backside. The being extended a hand to me. I frantically crab-crawled away from her. Pine needles and rocks cut into my hands but didn't slow me down.

"Celeste, wait." The creature spoke in a soft and whimsical voice.

It knows my name! my brain screamed. I flipped over onto my hands and knees, scraping at the ground, trying to get enough traction to bolt. A hand touched my shoulder, and I screamed for all I was worth. My body tensed. This was it. I was about to die.

The soothing voice tried to comfort me, "Shhh ... I am here to help you."

Like heck you are, I thought. Finally, I got my feet under me and ran. I made it two strides before an exposed tree root hindered my retreat. My foot caught. I went down. Hard. My head cracked against something rough and unyielding. Warmth ran down my forehead as my vision swam in and out of focus. The blurred face of the woman came into sight.

"We've been looking for you, Celeste. Your blood on the carving confirmed your identity. The changes will begin now. Not just for you, but for Gabe and Kendall as well. There is no stopping it. I am here to guide you, to help you." Her voice grew faint, like she was calling to me through a tunnel as I moved further and further away.

Then everything went black.

CHAPTER 5

 Celeste, can you hear me?"

Fabric ripped, water sloshed, something damp touched a spot on my forehead that sent darts of pain shooting through raw nerves.

My heavy eyes struggled open. "Alec?" I croaked.

"There you are." For reasons unbeknownst to me his voice was riddled with urgency. "Can you tell me what happened to you?"

"I ... was ... taking ... a nap." My tongue felt thick, causing my words to come out slow and slurred.

"You were taking a nap in the middle of the woods?"

I focused enough to make out the silhouette of trees above me. When had night fallen? I turned my head and nausea rolled my stomach. I groaned and squeezed my eyes shut, hoping it would stop the forest from spinning.

"Easy, now. No sudden moves. You may have a concussion. Do you know how you hit your head?" He dabbed at my forehead again, which sent fresh shock waves through it.

"Don't know. Had a weird dream …" I trailed off, unable to recall what it had been about.

"We need to get you out of here and have someone look you over. I'm going to pick you up. Will you be okay to move?"

The idea of motion angered my upset belly. "No … think I'm going to be sick."

"I know you feel like crap, but the gash on your head is bad. You're going to need stitches. Did you drive here?"

I tried to nod, but even that slight move caused another groan to escape me.

"Good. We're gonna head back to your car, okay?"

"Kay."

"Do me a favor," Alec said as he slid one arm under my knees and one under my shoulders. "Warn me before you puke. Here we go. Ready?"

"Mmm-hmm," was all I could muster.

As gently as he could, Alec lifted me up. My head rolled against his chest. The night breeze brushed over my skin and cooled my sore head. He did his best not to jostle me as he walked, but my stomach still gurgled in protest of the motion. As a frequent sufferer of motion sickness, I knew it would help to open my eyes. Alec's face was close enough to mine for me to notice a light dusting of freckles across his nose and the tops of his cheeks. I liked them. Almost as much as his pretty eyes.

"What were you doing out here?" I knew I sounded drunk but could do nothing to correct it.

"It's been a while since I've been home." Alec tossed me up a little bit to get a better grip. "I really missed hiking in the mountains. So, I decided to take advantage of the situation. I didn't even realize how far I'd gone until the sun started to set. I brought water but no flashlight. If you hadn't been in the clearing, I never would've seen you."

His mention of the clearing brought the flutter of a memory. A light so bright I had to shield my eyes. Then … nothing.

"Do you want me to try and walk?"

He gave me a half-grin despite the beads of sweat that dotted his forehead. "You weigh all of what, a buck-five? I think I can handle it."

When we arrived in the parking lot, Alec carefully lowered my feet to the ground. I was thankful for the arm he kept around my waist. My wobbly legs were threatening to give. "Where are your keys?"

My head still throbbed, but my case of cloudy brain had lessened. "In my satchel."

"Where's your satchel?"

I looked at the trail, then back to Alec.

"Crap."

"There's a spare key in the glove compartment. Doors are unlocked."

"Not safe, but helpful in this situation," Alec muttered as he opened the passenger side door and helped me in. He rolled my window down before shutting the door. I didn't mind. It might shake off the remaining fog in my brain. Alec climbed in and started the truck. I leaned my head against the seat and closed my eyes as he drove.

"The changes will start now, Celeste. Not just for you but for Gabe and Kendall as well."

My eyes snapped open. Those words! I remembered those words. Where had I heard them? Fear coiled in my stomach. I glanced around to see how close to Grams' we were.

"Where are you going!" I yelled over the whipping wind.

"To the ER to get your head stitched up."

I shook my head as adamantly as my current state would allow, "No. Take me home, please. Grams is a nurse. She'll take care of me."

"She's not going to put stitches in. And what if you have a concussion?"

"Please?" I have a slight fear of hospitals because there are

31

needles there. And I'm overwhelmingly, irrationally petrified of needles. "If she thinks I need to go, then I will. Okay?"

Alec frowned but did as I asked. He U-turned us back toward Grams'. No sooner had the truck pulled into the driveway than the front door flew open and Grams ran out. Gabe and Kendall trailed her.

Grams' face was a tight, stern mask of barely contained anger. The sight of me changed that.

"Sakes alive, Celeste! What happened to you?" She gripped my elbow and did a quick assessment of my visible injuries.

"I fell on the path and hit my head. Alec found me," I said.

Alec wasted no time. "I wanted to take her to the hospital and get her checked out, but she refused to go."

"Let's get her inside; I'll take a look at her. If she needs to go to the hospital, she will." Her tone left no room for argument. "I heard you were back in town, Alec. Thank you for coming to my granddaughter's rescue."

They hustled me inside to the downstairs bathroom. I avoided the mirror altogether. I wasn't ready for that train wreck yet. Kendall put the lid down on the toilet so I could sit. Grams grabbed a washcloth from under the sink and held it under the running water.

"This may sting," she warned. I concentrated on the mauve and burgundy swirls in the wallpaper to distract myself.

She dabbed at my head. To my surprise, it didn't hurt. Again she wiped and patted. Then she stopped. Her brow creased. She rinsed the washcloth and came at me once more. This time she swiped the cloth across my entire forehead.

Grams took a step back, her head cocked. "I don't understand where all the blood came from. Your scratch is already closed up."

"What? When I found her, her forehead was ripped open clear to the bone!" Alec pushed his way in to get a better look. I grimaced at his colorful choice of words.

Grams took a step back so Alec could see for himself. Crouched down in front of me, he grabbed my chin between his thumb and index finger. Confusion filled his face as he turned my head from side to side.

"That's not possible. It's just a scratch."

"Head wounds bleed like no other. It must've looked worse than it was," Grams explained.

Curiosity got the best of me. I pushed Alec's hand away and stood up to see for myself. I tried to keep my focus on only my forehead. Smack dab in the middle of my head was a small pink scratch. I ran my finger across it. The pain was gone. Even my headache had vanished. Alec was right. That didn't seem possible.

My eyes wandered to the rest of my appearance. I didn't know who the chick in the mirror with the crazed eyes was, but she was downright frightening. Trails of blood streaked my face and peppered the front of my shirt. The only clean part of me was where Grams tended to my scratch. Leaves, dirt, and pine needles covered me. I had a bird's nest for hair. Pretty. I reached for the faucet to wash away the grime. My extended hand stopped me short. It was filthy. Both of my hands were. Dirt was packed under my fingernails as if I'd been digging.

Or clawing at the ground.

The room shrunk around me. I remembered. I remembered everything. My breath came short and fast as panic bubbled through me. I could feel the concerned eyes of my family and friend burning into my skin. On the verge of losing it, I bolted from the room.

"I'm going to take a shower," I stated and ran up the stairs to our bathroom.

I didn't risk another look in the mirror but stripped off my soiled clothes and stepped into the shower. I turned the water as hot as I could stand it and scrubbed my skin raw with my loofah. I couldn't have seen what I thought I did. It was fodder for sci-fi movies, not real life. There had to be a rational explanation. There had to be. What did I know? I knew I hit my head, and I knew I was a chronic klutz. Maybe, just maybe, I confused the order of things. I could've fallen, in typical Celeste fashion, then dreamed the bird-woman.

I sighed and let the tension leave my body. Of course that was what happened. It made sense. I climbed out of the shower, toweled off, then pulled on my pajamas and went straight to bed. After I flicked off the light, I pulled the covers up to my ear. Nothing out of the ordinary had happened other than a wickedly vivid dream. And if I told myself that enough, maybe it would remove that lingering doubt that tugged at the back of my mind.

Worried I may have a concussion, Grams came to check on me frequently throughout the night. Each time she found me awake, staring into the darkness. I couldn't fool myself no matter how hard I tried. I knew what I had seen.

CHAPTER 6

B_y the early hours of the following morning, Grams determined I was fine and left me alone to rest. Once sleep finally got a hold of me, it didn't want to let go. I slept the entire day away and woke as the sun was beginning to set.

I stumbled downstairs to find an empty house. According to the note Grams left me on the dining room table, Kendall was at Keith's, Gabe was at football practice, and she had gone to Opry Land with her Red Hat Society friends for the weekend. She assured me she could be back in an instant if I needed her, but that was the last thing I wanted. After last night's ordeal, I didn't want anyone hovering over me, watching my every move. I needed normalcy. Time alone with my thoughts to convince myself I hadn't gone completely loony.

I poured myself a bowl of cereal and thumbed through the packet of information that came in the mail from Rhodes College. The campus was beautiful. All the buildings were stone with elaborate archways and impressive moldings. They looked like undersized castles. I tried to envision what my life would be like there. Cramming for exams in the library. Meeting friends at the Lynx Lair for lunch. Taking in a little culture at the gorgeous theater. A wonderful adventure, far away from weird birds that cause hallucinations.

Halfway through my second bowl of Fruity Pebbles, my belly began to flutter. Worried the milk may've been past its prime, I took some deep breaths and gave my stomach a chance to settle.

Instead of the problem correcting itself, it got worse. My heart began to pound like a jackhammer. My pulse thudded in my veins. I felt...agitated. I was frustrated and angry for no reason whatsoever. I couldn't sit still. I wrung my hands as I paced from the kitchen to the living room and back again. My jaw tensed to the point of pain.

The front door squeaked open. Hoping it was someone breaking in that I could unleash this fury on, I stalked toward the foyer.

Gabe intercepted me when he rounded the corner into the living room. "Hey."

It hit me like a punch to the gut, the emotions I felt were coming from him. I could feel what he was feeling, and he was radiating anger.

"Are you okay?" I snapped. At my abrupt tone, Gabe's chestnut eyes widened and his eyebrows rose.

"Yeah ... why?" he asked slowly.

"You seem upset!"

Gabe laughed while giving me a 'my sister's done lost her damned mind' look. "No. I just walked in the door. You, on the other hand, are wound pretty tight."

"I'm fine!" I barked. "Did something happen at practice?"

"Nope. What's with you?"

"Nothing's wrong with me. What are you so ticked about?"

"I'm not ticked about anything." His voice started to echo the emotion coming off of him. I briefly considered that I may be causing this.

"You're obviously angry. Now what's going on?" I blurted out, my hands balled into fists.

His wide jaw clenched. "Did that bump on the head damage your hearing? I said I'm fine."

"You're not upset?"

"No more than usual," he muttered. "We done here?"

"Yeah." My voice was barely a whisper, but my heart pounded away at top speed. I had no idea what was happening to me. I needed some distance to figure it out. "I think I'm going to go lay down for a bit."

"Good." he grumbled and turned his back on me as he stomped to the kitchen.

I fled the intrusive emotion and retreated to the safe confines of my room. As the door slammed behind me, I collapsed against it. Distance muffled Gabe's emotion. I was back to feeling just annoyed instead of fuming.

I breathed a sigh of relief and pushed off the door. Two strides across the room and a flash of red caught my eye. There was something on my pillow that had most definitely *not* been there before. A scroll, its leathery paper yellow with age, sat where my head had been a short time before. The red, silk ribbon that decorated it made it look like a gift. An offering.

My eyes darted around nervously. Someone had been in our room. Were they still here? I looked around for something to use as a bludgeoning device, just in case. A purple polka-dotted lamp isn't high on the list of intimidating weapons, but it was all I had. I snuck up to the closet, flung open the door, and stabbed my lamp inside. Nothing but clothes. I crouched down and swung my lamp wildly under my bed, then Kendall's. When I came up empty-handed again, I walked over to the window. Unlocked. Whoever left my little present could've snuck in and out easily. Especially if said person had wings...

I stared at the paper like it was going to jump up and bite me.

Which it might. Weirder things had happened lately. My hesitant feet scuffed against the floor as I forced myself toward the mysterious parchment. With a trembling hand, I grasped the scroll. I freed it from the silky ribbon, then unrolled the thick paper. At the top of the page, etched in a dramatic cursive, were the words:

Power of the Empathe

Beneath that were answers to questions I hadn't known to ask.

The empathe feels the emotions of others. This power is meant to guide by "listening" to those in need of aid. Once the ability is activated, its power can be difficult to endure. For the weak-minded, every emotion will feel crushing. Ultimately, the fragile mind will collapse. Only through strong-will and control will you survive it.

I glanced up at the gryphon statue on my nightstand. "Is this your idea of a love note?"

I had an inkling of an idea where the scroll came from. But no way was I ready to let my mind go there. Instead, I focused on the message. An uplifting note it was not. I like my mind. As a rule, I didn't want it to collapse.

I flopped back on my bed and stared up at the ceiling. At this distance, Gabe's anger wasn't too bad. It kind of felt like when I went on one of my caffeine binges and my insides got all jittery. But if I was going to get a handle on this, I'd have to do it at a closer proximity. It seemed like a good idea, though, to wait until Gabe got over his male PMS. While I had nothing to base this theory on, I assumed less hostility would make it easier. Maybe.

As soon as I had that thought my heart seemed to swell in my chest. Light and warmth filled me. It was wonderful. It wasn't mine. I could still feel Gabe's anger, but now it was mixed with this wonderful, new feeling. What could possibly be making my big, macho brother feel all warm and mushy? Nosiness got the best of me. I had to know. Sure, curiosity killed the cat. But really, what was the worst that could happen?

CHAPTER 7

A smarter person would've cautiously treaded into these potentially dangerous waters, but I never claimed to be smart. I thundered down the stairs completely unaware of the mind-blowing, gut-wrenching, indescribable pain in store for me. Oh, how quickly I learned.

I expected Gabe's emotions. They were unpleasant, but I knew they were coming. Naive girl that I am, I hadn't considered the possibility of another person being there. Kendall's presence blindsided me. The flutter I first felt was just the beginning. My heart swam in what I can only describe as love in its purest and most genuine form. It would've been a beautiful feeling to bask in, if Gabe's anger hadn't tainted it. Together they created a perfect storm of emotions.

I barely made it off the stairs before the torturous mix seized me. Gasping, I grasped at my chest. It felt as though someone was carving out my heart with a dull blade and flushing the wound with hot molten lava. I wanted to run, but the pain paralyzed me.

Tears streamed down my face. I was incapacitated by emotions that weren't even mine.

"Celeste!" Keni ran to me and felt my face for a fever. I jerked at her touch. It amplified her emotion. "Gabe, there's something wrong with her!"

Gabe's head whipped in our direction. He sprinted to my side and grabbed my arm to steady me. "She was acting weird earlier. Is she having a seizure or something?"

Their combined touch caused a monsoon of emotion to ravage me. My body convulsed under the weight of it.

I couldn't breathe.

Couldn't speak.

Couldn't think of anything but the agony.

Their emotions were killing me.

"Go get her a cold cloth and a glass of water!" Gabe barked.

Keni dashed to the kitchen. Her distance gave me just enough of a break. I inhaled a deep, jagged breath. As the oxygen rushed back to my brain, it screamed at me: *She'll be right back! Run!*

I shoved my brother out of the way with a force that knocked him to the ground and bolted straight for the back door without stopping. If they called to me, I didn't hear it. My mind screamed to be free. My hands grappled to turn the knob. Finally winning, I hurled the door open. It rattled on its hinges. I darted out into the cool night air and didn't stop until I reached the wooden fence at the back of Grams' small yard. I fell against it and slid to the ground. I gasped for breath and willed my pounding heart to steady its beat.

I could still feel Gabe and Kendall's emotions, but they were muted. With my head leaned back against the fence, I took deep breaths until the synchronized pounding of my head and chest slowed.

"Celeste? Are you okay?" Keni called from the doorway, then stepped out into the yard. Her concern caused fresh bubbles to churn my stomach and a dull ache to begin in my heart.

"Stop!" She froze. I tried to steady my quaking voice when I added, "I just needed some air."

"Are you coming in?"

The mere thought of that was almost vomit-worthy. Inside meant another emotional lashing. Outside was peace. "I think I'm going to sleep in the tree house tonight."

Her giddy excitement bounced into me. "Like we did when we were little! We haven't done that in, like, forever! I'll go get us some sleeping bags and pillows."

"No!" I snapped way too sharply. Softening my tone as best I could, I explained. "I kind of just want some alone time."

Her cloud of disappointment shaded my heart.

"Whatever ... didn't want to anyway." She sulked, then turned to march inside and pout.

"Wait, Keni." I felt her hopes rise as she turned, which made what I had to ask that much worse. "Could you still bring me out a sleeping bag and my pillow?"

I got to experience firsthand the sting of my words. I was a horrible human being. Any other person would've told me where I could stick that sleeping bag. But Keni wasn't capable of that kind of hostility.

"Fine. I'll be right back," she grumbled. True to her word, a few minutes later she deposited a sleeping bag and my pillow right outside the door.

For the next two days, I holed up in the child-sized tree house. Initially, I stayed there out of fear of a repeat emotional overexposure. Then it became my goal to learn to control this empathe thing, or suffer a complete mental breakdown trying. How's that for positive thinking? Gabe and Keni came out to check on me a few times. Each time I offered up some lame excuse about camping and barked at them to go away. That wouldn't have worked on Grams. Good thing she was out of town. Only when they were gone or sleeping would I sneak inside for food and to heed nature's call. Through trial and error, I figured out how to block out their intrusive emotions. After that, the feelings only came to me when I wanted them to. I could channel one of my siblings and draw their essence to me. Which was pretty friggin' cool. However, all these experiments happened from my tree house sanctuary. There was no telling how I would handle another face to face interaction, or venturing out in public. Dread over what might happen made me stay in my tree.

My solitude ended as soon as Grams came home. The back door was flung open, and Grams stomped across the yard. Panic knotted my stomach. I couldn't lose control in front of her. I just couldn't.

She stopped at the bottom of the ladder and glared up at me. Through clenched teeth she hissed, "Celeste Garrett, what is the matter with you? Your sister told me you haven't left this tree house for two days? And the neighbors called and complained that you were out here talking to yourself all hours of the day and night." *I was? Hmm, I had no idea.* "Have ya lost your mind?"

Grams was clearly ticked, but I couldn't feel it. An unintentional giggle escaped me. Just to see if I could, I concentrated and sought out her feelings. There they were! She was perturbed ... and more than a little concerned. Odd, her anger was growing. Yikes! She was turning into a red hot ball of cranky! It occurred to me that the cause was probably her idiot granddaughter wordlessly staring at her with a big, dopey grin on her face. I quickly blinked and disconnected our emotional tie.

"I was just enjoying the beautiful Tennessee scenery, Grams." I smoothed my hair behind my ears and tried to look less like a raving lunatic.

"And the talkin' to yourself?"

"Didn't realize I was," I giggled nervously. "But we all do that from time to time, don't we?"

"I guess so. We don't normally carry on entire conversations though." Her eyes stayed narrowed. She was nowhere near convinced.

"How about if I come inside for dinner?" A risky but mandatory move.

"That would be nice."

"Great. I'll fold up my sleeping bag and be inside in just a minute."

"Good." As she walked back to the house, she muttered to herself. "Kids acting like they're on drugs. Back in my day, you didn't act like that. You'd wind up in some loony bin. Doesn't think I'll send her butt there? Darn right I will! Talking to herself! Who in their right mind talks to themself?!"

As I picked up my stuff, I braced myself for whatever would befall me inside. I stepped into the house expecting the very worst. What I found instead was Grams pulling containers out of a KFC bag, Keni setting the table, Gabe pouring four glasses of milk, and all outside emotions staying perfectly at bay.

Gabe glanced up and grinned. "Hey, she returns! Enjoy your time roughing it?"

"Yeah, it was … enlightening." I washed my hands in the sink, then took my seat at the table.

Kendall cringed and waved her hand in front of her face. "You know, when you get in touch with nature, it's still okay to shower."

"Noted." I laughed. "I'll take care of that right after dinner."

We dove into the delicious spread before us, and no one pried any further into my backyard shenanigans. As relieved as I was to have a handle on this, I wasn't convinced my good luck would hold out. These were controlled circumstances. I still had no idea how I would fare around strangers. It could send me over the edge, never to return. Unfortunately, there was only one way to find out.

CHAPTER 8

I had a plan. I was fairly certain it was an asinine plan, but it was all I could come up with, so I was gonna own it. Since my head versus rock incident, Alec had called, texted, and stopped by repeatedly to check on me. In his latest text, he asked me out for dinner. I couldn't deny that I wanted to see him again, plus I needed to try out my empathe ability in the big, wide world. (Well, not the big world—more the Podunk, isolated world—but still.) The worst that could happen was me being unable to hold back the emotions that invaded me, then having myself a fun little freak out in front of the cute boy. Heck, I might even lose control of a few bodily functions in front of him. That'd be swell. If things went that route, my plan was to claim food poisoning and run like that rumored panther was chasing me. See? I had a plan.

I inhaled a shaky breath to calm my nerves and exhaled through pursed, freshly glossed lips. I had scoured my closet for the right ensemble for tonight. I wanted an outfit that said, "I like you, but I don't know how much yet. So, I want to entice you without leading you on." Nothing in my closet fit that description. There was no choice but to call in Kendall's keen fashion sense. She dressed me in a pair of blue jean capris and a loosely fitted canary yellow tank top with lace trim at the neckline. Then she came at me baring her tackle box full of hair pins, combs, and other frilly paraphernalia. I repelled her by holding up her only known weakness—a scrunchie I fully intended to use to pull my hair back. She hissed and retreated to her perfectly quaffed shadows. I checked out my reflection in the mirror. Nice and casual. No way could Alec get the wrong idea.

"*Celeste*! Your boyfriend's here!" Gabe bellowed from the bottom of the stairs.

Gabe Garrett, you are a monumental pain in my...

I did my best to ignore his flare up of foot-in-mouth disease and focused instead on bracing myself for whatever the night would hold. I flung the bedroom door open with as much courage as I could muster and headed downstairs. An unforeseen problem developed as soon as my feet touched the polished wooden stairs. I began envisioning all sorts of terrible scenarios. What if I read Alec's emotions and found out he didn't like me? Or that he's only after "one thing"? What if half way through the night he decides I'm a total goober and I just so happen to be plugged into his emotions at the moment he makes that discovery? Worse yet, what if he's only using me to get closer to Kendall? It wouldn't be the first time that happened. I hadn't even thought about the consequences of knowing exactly what he was feeling! Why did I think I could pull this off?!

By the time I reached the bottom of the stairs, I had worked myself up into a state of sweaty, frazzled panic. Worse yet, I couldn't will myself to round the corner into the foyer. I was stuck at the bottom of the stairwell with my legs sending a message loud and clear: this is going to be unpleasant. Therefore we have decided against going. Thank you very much for the offer, but no.

Idle conversation from the other side of the wall. "What are you ... lifting twenty-four/seven? You're really bulking up. I almost didn't recognize you."

"No, I haven't been hitting the weights any more than usual. Must just be from working out with the team."

Listen to them, chattering away while I'm stuck mid-panic attack. I knew I was being ridiculous. If my stubborn, lead feet wouldn't budge, I was just going to move them manually. I grabbed the corner of the wall in a white-knuckled grip and hoisted myself around into the foyer in one big swoop. Alec and Gabe stopped and stared.

"Everything okay?" Alec asked, his eyes wide and alarmed.

I didn't know yet ... was it? It might take a second before it hits. I wasn't feeling anything. Nothing rushed over me. The rule must apply to other people too! The emotions would only come to me if I reached out for them. Relief flooded me—immediately followed by embarrassment.

I still had a grip on the wall like I was bracing myself for some sort of natural disaster. With the hold I had, it was impressive I didn't crack the plaster. I quickly let go, adjusted my posture, and crammed my hands into my pockets.

"Sorry. I ... thought I left my flat iron on upstairs," I stammered. I'm an awful liar.

"And it caused the second story to explode? What is with you lately?" Gabe's dark brows pulled together as he frowned.

I tittered a weak laugh to make light of it. "Yeah, funny, huh? Hi, Alec."

The unanswered questions that played across his face made me glad I didn't have to feel his emotions right then. The expression he settled on was equal parts amusement and confusion. "Hi. Nice entrance."

"Like that? Wait till you see my dinner show."

Gabe turned to Alec and clasped a hand on his shoulder with enough force to cause Alec to wince. "You know, no one will think badly of you if you decide not to go through with this. We know how she is and would totally understand."

I glared daggers at him.

"I'll take my chances." Alec winked at me with a crooked grin.

"Whatever, man. Your funeral." As Gabe passed me, he noticed my evil eye and answered it with a toothy grin. My rebuttal was an elbow to his ribs, which hurt like I'd rammed my funny bone into a brick wall. I grabbed my elbow and grimaced in pain. Gabe laughed.

With my brother gone, Alec moved in closer. He put a hand on each side of my head and did a mock examination, turning my head this way and that. He then turned his attention to my left arm, gently lifting it up, flipping it over, inspecting it, and then dropping it back to my side. He repeated the pattern with my right arm and paused to dot a kiss to the elbow that was smarting from hitting Gabe.

"What are you doing?" I asked.

"Making sure you're still structurally sound after your head trauma." He held my hand in both of his for a moment before reluctantly releasing it. "You seem good."

"I'm feeling better. But thank you for the clean bill of health."

He looked into my eyes intently. "You're good? Really?"

I could feel myself blushing under his intense stare. I broke our gaze and looked away as I pushed a loose lock of hair behind my ear. "Yes, I'm really okay. How've you been?"

Alec filled me in on his activities over the last few days. I'll be honest. I completely tuned out. Despite my earlier fears, curiosity got the best of me. I opened myself up to whatever his psyche would tell me.

It came so subtly I almost missed it. My palms dampened, my heartbeat sped up a bit, and a fresh blush colored my face. He liked me, and I was feeling just how much. Guilt plagued me because I didn't know if my feelings matched his. Truth be told, I'd only ever had one boyfriend. His name was Owen. We met in art class and I fell for his soulful brown eyes and easy smile. Right about the time in our relationship when we were thinking of exploring "second base," my Dad died. Owen tried to comfort me and be there for me, but I completely shut him out. When I found taking care of my family left no time for anything else, I broke up with him. Since then, I hadn't dated at all. I didn't know if I was ready for another relationship or not. I definitely didn't want to hurt Alec like I had Owen.

Yet as I stood there, deeply immersed in these borrowed emotions, I couldn't help but revel in how nice it felt. This level of enamored infatuation made me feel alive again, even if it wasn't my emotion to hold onto. As I looked at Alec, the feelings of adoration accentuated all his finest attributes. His crystal blue eyes twinkled like that of a mischievous little boy. The afternoon light filtering in through the window emphasized the red in his hair. If I kept plugged into him like this, I was going to have no choice but to stretch up on my tiptoes and gently press my lips to his.

But I didn't.

Instead, I closed the valve on the emotional spigot that flowed from him and went back to my own infuriatingly indecisive feelings.

"... it came out blue, which was weird. But I think I can live with it." Wrong moment to tune back in. I had no clue what he was talking about.

"Blue's not bad." I interjected, hoping the answer would fit somehow.

"Absolutely. Blue is totally workable." His eyes crinkled as he grinned. I gave an internal phew and vowed not to let my mind wander like that again. "So, are you hungry?"

"Famished. Let's eat."

***

The Old Shamrock Bar and Grill located on Gore Avenue was more bar and less grill. Sunlight had no place here. The lone window at the front of the narrow establishment had a blackout curtain over it to keep out the offending light. It was only seven o'clock, yet within the confines of these walls, darkness was a permanent resident. Regulations on smoking hadn't reached this corner of the world. A thick haze of nicotine hung heavy in the air. An old juke box in the corner played a song from the eighties that I had heard my mom hum a few times. I think the musician was the prince of something, though I had no idea of what. On the scuffed-up wood floor, couples swayed. There were maybe eighteen people there, which wasn't a bad turn out for a town the size of a postage stamp. We were the youngest people there by a good twenty years.

My apprehension eased when I found that, just like with Alec, no emotions invaded me. I was free to relax. We took a seat at a tattered, round table and ordered a couple of burgers with sodas. As we waited for our food, Alec filled me in on his life back in Nashville.

"I'm actually an intern at the station right now, which means they work me to death and pay me pretty much nothing. But I'm hoping when I get my degree, they'll keep me on. Maybe even start paying me enough that I won't need to have three roommates just to make rent."

"Cozy."

"Nope, not at all. But it's better than living on campus."

"Easy on the horror stories, that'll be me in September." The waitress arrived with our burgers and we dug in.

"No, it really is a good experience. It can just get kind of crazy. Don't expect to have any kind of privacy while you're there. But you'll meet some cool people and have a lot of fun. What school are you going to?" Alec asked through his mouthful.

I paused to swallow the huge bite I'd taken. "Rhodes College in Memphis."

"I heard that's a really good school. Beautiful campus."

"It looks beautiful in the pictures." I grabbed my napkin and wiped a mound of ketchup off my face. "I haven't seen it in person yet."

"Have you picked a major?"

I grabbed the salt shaker to season my fries. "I want to be an art teacher." Alec gave an appreciative nod as he slugged down his drink. "So, how are you liking being in front of the camera? Is this a permanent change?"

"I never wanted it to be, but I'm enjoying it. It's exciting. I get to interview people, hunt for leads, even save the occasional damsel in distress." He met my eye and graced me with another of his charming grins. I felt myself blush but doubted Alec could tell in the dim lighting.

"What've you learned about the fabled panther of Gainesboro?"

His eyes sparked at the mention of his story. He wiped his mouth and then leaned forward to rest his elbows on the table. "It's really getting interesting. There have been three different sightings. Two of them were hikers in the mountains. One in broad daylight. They got a really good look and swear it's a black panther. The third sighting though I'm convinced is a hoax."

"Why's that?"

"It was at a house on the outskirts of town, right at the base of the mountains. A little boy, I think he was like eight or nine, says he saw the panther. According to him he woke up and it was staring into his room with its front paws pressed up against the glass of his window."

I imagined waking up and seeing a gigantic cat with razor sharp teeth staring at me. The bed would need new sheets. "That would be terrifying!"

"Yeah, it would be if it actually happened. But last time I checked panthers aren't really known for their peeping habits. Not to mention, I scoped the house out. With the height of the window the panther would've had to stand on its hind legs. That's just not realistic for a panther on the prowl. More likely, the kid heard some gossip about the sightings and made up a story to get attention." He gave a dismissive shrug. "Either way, until I get some actual pictures, all the sightings are alleged. Now if I could get some actual footage, my producer at the station would love that!"

"You might even get promoted up from intern to ... hmmm, what's a step up from an intern? Janitor?" I teased.

He grinned and threw his napkin at me. "Laugh all you want, freshman. You'll be in the intern trenches before you know it."

"I know." I raised the back of my hand to my head in a melodramatic gesture of despair. Then, trying to sound casual but failing miserably, I asked, "How long do you think the story will keep you in Gainesboro?"

"Like having me around, do ya?" Alec wiggled his eyebrows at me.

My mouth opened but only, "I...uh...um..." came out.

Alec laughed and rose from the table. "You think about it. I'm going to go take care of the bill. Maybe you can have an answer formulated by the time I get back."

As soon as he walked away, I smacked myself in the head for being such a doofus. It was a good thing Alec was a cool guy that didn't seem fazed by my Celeste-isms. I settled back into my chair and waited for him to come back. Gazing around the bar, I reveled in how nice it was to be out having a normal evening. I hadn't even thought about my new ability.

Until now.

The room was full of unsuspecting people chock full of all sorts of emotions. I couldn't help but wonder what it would hurt to take a little peek. In an incredibly bad move, I started with the bleached blonde woman in stonewashed jeans grinding against her boyfriend on the dance floor.

Whoa! That's not pretty! She has some plans for that guy! I quickly snapped off the connection. Unfortunately, not before I got a mental picture that I really didn't want.

Feeling a little gun shy, I decided to go a less traumatizing route. Our waitress seemed like a safe choice. She looked exhausted and was covered in a sheen of sweat. Her emotions were pretty straightforward; she felt overworked and underpaid. The man behind the bar became my next target. He was incredibly stressed and suffering from a sharp pain in his abdomen. Judging by the level of his anxiety, I was betting it was an ulcer. He should really have that looked at.

I looked around for someone else to aim my ability at. The man leaning against the bar looked promising. He was definitely on the prowl. His tan cowboy hat was pushed down over his eyes. His shiny blue shirt was unbuttoned to the middle of his chest and a shock of black chest hair sprung out. A thick, gold rope chain hung around his neck but vanished into his mass of body hair. His tongue fiddled wildly with the toothpick protruding from his mouth. He probably thought it was sexy. It wasn't. It was gross. His head bobbed along to the music as he scanned the room.

Maybe I could find out who he's planning to hit on and warn them. I giggled then opened up the channel to the cowboy.

The emotion that hit me wasn't his. My head whipped toward the door. It came from out there. My heart clenched in someone else's crushing terror. Whoever it was didn't know if they would live or die.

My chair clattered to the ground as I sprang up.

CHAPTER 9

Y ou all right?" Alec stood behind me, righting my chair.

"There's something happening," I murmured and headed for the door, oblivious to whether or not Alec followed. As soon as I stepped outside, it felt like someone lassoed my heart and yanked it toward the mountains. I cast my eyes in that direction but saw nothing out of the ordinary.

Alec kept pace with me. "Did you hear or see something?"

That seemed an easier explanation, so I nodded. "Whatever it is, it's that way."

"What is it that we're looking for?"

"I don't really—" A gunshot pierced through the night and cut off my words.

Instantly, Alec was all business. "That was in town. It couldn't have been too far from here. I'll go get my car." He sprinted off toward the parking lot.

The wheels in my head turned at a dizzying speed. A gunshot put a terrifying spin on this. Was I being drawn toward a homicidal maniac? I wasn't equipped to take on a gun-wielding nut. What was I going to do? Tune into his emotions and try to rationalize with him? *I know you feel you need to go on a crazed killing spree, but I'd like to discuss why.* Yeah, not so helpful.

Police sirens interrupted that frightening line of thought as two patrol cars whipped passed me. The men in blue would get there before I did. Good. They have guns and stuff to actually handle situations like this.

Alec's lime green Volkswagen Thing screeched to a halt in front of me. He chattered away like an excited little howler monkey while I wedged myself into his shoebox-sized car. "Wow, I guess you were right! Maybe it's the panther. Ugh—I don't have the video camera. But if it's still there, I could probably get some footage on my phone."

"Fingers crossed." My tone didn't reflect his enthusiasm.

Alec floored it as much as his car's lawn-mower engine would allow and steered us in the direction the cops went. They turned, but neither of us saw where. He veered to the right at the first crossroad we came to.

"Wait!" I slapped my hand against the dashboard.

Alec slammed on the brakes. Thankfully, there wasn't a car behind us. "What?"

I closed my eyes and tuned into the feeling. "The next street up, turn left."

"Can you hear the sirens or something?"

"Just go!"

I didn't have to ask twice. The tiny car whirred off as Alec followed my directions. As soon as we turned, the red and blue flashing lights came into view.

"Geez, you must have like supersonic hearing!" He practically bounced in his seat as he threw his Thing in park.

"It was just a lucky guess."

"Let me know if you have any lucky guesses about lottery numbers, okay?"

"Sure thing." We climbed out of the car onto a street very similar to Grams'. Modest homes lined both sides of the road. The spectacle centered around a beige two story with a wraparound porch.

Two officers rounded the side of the house toward the backyard with their guns drawn. In the driveway, a man I guessed to be in his thirties screamed until he was red in the face at another pair of officers.

"That thing was in my yard! How do you explain that? What if my daughter had been out there? She's only eight! She could've been killed! Now I wanna know what you're—" he jabbed a finger at one of the officers "—gonna do about it."

The officer's answer came in a hushed tone that I couldn't hear.

"It *is* another panther sighting! Great job, Celeste!" Alec slapped me on the back. "You ever thought about a career as a reporter?"

"Not really, no."

"Well, you should! I'm going to move in a little closer and see if I can get an interview with the witness. Stay here, okay?" And he was off. For someone who was forced into the reporter role, he took to it with vigor.

The two officers came back from behind the house holstering their weapons. The younger of the two shouted for all to hear, "There's nothing back there now."

Many of the on-lookers groaned their disappointment then disappeared back inside their homes. The crowd thinned out quickly now that the show was over.

I stayed for two reasons, the first being that my ride home just ran off. The second was the force I didn't understand that drew me here. Since the first reason might be a while, I decided to explore the second. I centered myself and opened the channel. My feet instinctively moved, following the navigation of my heart. A tightening vise grip of cold, hard fear led me across the yard, up the stairs, and onto the porch.

At first glance the porch seemed empty until something shifted behind the white-washed porch swing. I crept forward all the while chanting, "Please don't be a panther, please don't be a panther" to myself. I held my breath, bent down, and peeked with one eye open and the other squeezed shut. My other eye snapped open, and I expelled my breath. Huddled in the corner sat a little girl. She hugged her knees to her chest with trembling arms. Her forehead rested on her knees. A curtain of long, chestnut hair shielded her face.

The last thing I wanted to do was frighten her further. "Hi there," I whispered.

Her head came up gradually, as if she was scared of what she would see. Her big, brown eyes were red-rimmed with tears. "Is it gone?"

"The panther?"

She nodded her confirmation.

"Yeah, it's gone." I gave her my best reassuring smile. "I'm Celeste. What's your name?"

"Ella," she hiccupped.

"Well, Ella, the coast is clear now. So, how about if I take you over to your dad?"

"Is the mean man gone too?" Icy fear danced down my spine. The thought of someone hurting this sweet, little girl, or any child for that matter, revolted me.

"There was a man here?" I tried to keep my tone light.

She nodded, her lip quivering.

Did the panther belong to someone? I'd have to ask Alec if any of the other witnesses mentioned a man with the cat. "Did this man hurt you, Ella?"

"No. But he was going to." The certainty in her voice was chilling.

I plastered on a smile I definitely wasn't feeling and extended my hand to her. "Whoever it was is gone now. It's safe to come out."

Warily, she took it and let me guide her out of her hiding place.

I helped her up onto the floral print cushion of the swing and then took her hands in mine. "Do you think you could tell the nice police officers what happened?"

Her hair fanned out around her as she shook her head vigorously from side to side.

"Why not, sweetheart?"

"Cause I wasn't supposed to be outside. I was supposed to be in bed. If I tell them, they'll tell Daddy and Mommy and I'll get in trouble." Fresh tears sprang to her eyes.

"Okay, we won't talk to the officers," I reassured her. "Could you at least tell me?"

She dried her eyes on the back of her hand. "I wasn't sleepy, so I took my baby doll outside. I was showing her the stars like Mommy does with me. That's when I saw the man. He had scary eyes. They were black. He started asking me all sorts of questions."

"What kind of questions?"

"Stuff I didn't understand. He asked me if I was the...the one. If I had the power. I didn't know what he meant. I told him I didn't understand. That made him laugh, but it wasn't a nice laugh. He said he knew how to find out for sure. Then he disappeared and the panther came." Tears zigzagged down her flushed cheeks.

"He sicced his panther on you?" My astonishment caused my voice to come out a high-pitched squeak.

She gazed up at me as if contemplating a painful truth and shook her head. "I don't think so." She lowered her voice to a soft, barely-audible whisper. This confidential secret was meant solely for me. "I think he was the panther."

The image of the eagle transforming into a woman flashed before my eyes. There had to be a connection. It was too much of a coincidence. "What happened next?" I croaked.

"Daddy came outside with his gun. He saw the cat but not me. He shot at it and I ran and hid. I dropped my baby doll in the backyard," she sobbed.

I cupped Ella's face in my hands and wiped her tears away with my thumbs. "Shh, shh, shh. That man won't bother you again. I promise. I'll make sure he can never hurt you or threaten you again." I had no idea how I intended to keep that promise, but I felt compelled to say it. "And we'll find your dolly."

I held up my little finger to pinkie swear on it. As she linked her finger with mine, I opened the link between us. I needed to know she was okay. Her knot of fear loosened then fell away. For a split second I got the crazy notion that I had altered her emotions somehow. Huh.

Ella cocked her head to the side and peered up at me. "It's you, isn't it?"

"What's me?"

"You're the one he was looking for."

A simple sentence spoken from the innocent mind of a child, yet all the weird stuff compiling around me added a weight of believability to it. "I ... I think I might be."

She graced me with an angelic grin. "You'll stop him, Celeste. I know you will." At least one of us had faith in me.

My time with Ella came to an abrupt end when the front door of the house flew open and a frantic looking woman in her bathrobe raced out. "Ray! Ray! Ella's not in her room! And I found this in the backyard!" She raised a baby doll up for her husband to see.

"My Cindy doll!" Ella chirped.

The woman's head swiveled to Ella and me. Relief cast her eyes to the heavens and her hands to cover her heart. "Oh, thank you, God!" She rushed to Ella's side where she scooped her daughter up and showered her with kisses. "Don't you ever scare me like that again!"

"I'm sorry, Momma." Ella hugged her mother, and Cindy, tightly.

Ray, Alec, and the police officers joined us on the porch. Making sure little Ella was safe trumped everything else.

Ella's mother turned to me. "Thank you for finding her. Where was she?"

"She was here on the porch; she didn't get far."

"You must be new to town. I don't think we've met."

Ella twirled Cindy's hair around her finger. "That's Celeste, Momma. She's gonna catch the panther."

Funny how seven different adults could all give me the same patronizing look.

"Are you an avid large game hunter, Celeste?" Ray smirked. Alec and the officers snickered behind their hands. Heat rose to my cheeks.

Ella's mother elbowed her husband, "Be nice. She probably said that to calm your child down, you big jerk."

Ray bowed his head at his wife's comment. "You're right." He extended his hand to me. "I'm sorry, Celeste. Thank you for your help."

"It was no problem. She's a great kid."

He turned to the officers. "If we're done here, my wife and I need to put our little peanut to bed."

With one last wave to Ella, we said our goodbyes. Back in the car Alec was in overdrive. "I can't thank you enough for bringing me here! This is really going to help my story. I may have to keep you around. You're great for my career!"

Aren't those just the romantic words every girl longs to hear.

I ignored his comment. "Did any of the other witnesses mention seeing a man with the panther?"

"Ray didn't see anyone with the panther." His excitement deflated at my abrupt tone.

"No, but his daughter did."

Alec shook his head as if my poor, simple mind saddened him. "Celeste, there were people everywhere. She probably just told you that to get attention. Ray said when he was outside with the panther, his family was safely inside."

I gritted my teeth and tried not to slug him. "He didn't know she was out there. But she was. And she saw the panther, too. Only she said there was a man with him. Did anyone else mention that?"

"Well, yeah," he snorted. "You remember the little boy that said the panther was 'peeking' in his window?" He air quoted the word.

"Yeah?" My stomach churned. Another child was involved.

"He said that as the panther looked at him, it changed. It became a man. Like I said, he obviously had an active imagination and was using it to get attention. That's all Ella was doing, too. It worked on you because you're a kind-hearted, trusting person."

I wasn't even pretending to listen anymore. Two children had been targeted by this man-beast. If I was the one he was looking for, why was he harassing kids? My list of questions continued to grow, and I had nothing in the way of answers. I peered out at the mountain range veiled by the darkness of night. I had an idea where I needed to go. But first, I had to round up Gabe and Kendall. Somehow this involved them, too.

CHAPTER 10

No sooner had I stepped into the house then Grams cornered me in the foyer. "Celeste! There you are! You got a sec?"

Not really Grandmother, you see I'm currently investigating shapeshifting people. "Sure, what's up?" I put on a smile and hid any exasperation that tried to sneak into my voice.

A worried frown creased her face. "It's about your brother."

"Gabe?"

"Do you have another brother I don't know about?"

"No, of course not. What about him?"

Her eyebrows raised in disbelief. "What about him? You haven't noticed?"

Was his anger evident to everyone else, too? Maybe other people didn't need to be clairvoyant to see all the festering feelings he had bottled up. "You mean his mood? Yeah, I've tried to talk to him, but you know how he is..."

"No. His mood has been fine." She swatted my words away like flies. "It's his recent...growth."

"What?" Gabe reached his full height of six foot two when he was seventeen. Twenty seemed late for a growth spurt.

Grams' eyes widened and made her fake lashes tickle her forehead. "Celeste, how could you not have noticed? He's *huge*! I'm worried that he might be using...steroids." Unable to speak the last word out loud, she mouthed it to me.

I shook my head. "No. No way. He would never do something that stupid."

"But to bulk up that much in such a short amount of time? I don't know what else it could be. If that is what's going on, we need to get him some help. Slap him upside the head first, but then get him some help."

Now that she mentioned it, I remembered Alec making a comment about Gabe's size, too. And "roid rage" would explain the constant anger I felt from him. My field trip was going to have to wait fifteen minutes. I had to get to the bottom of this first and put Grams' mind at ease.

"I'll go talk to him and see if I can find anything out."

She smiled at me and gently touched the side of my face with her palm. "Thank you, honey. You're such a good girl. More so when you're not in a tree scaring the neighbors." With that she walked out the door I had just come in. "I'm off to bingo. Night!"

I vigorously rubbed my hands over my face. As if I didn't have enough on my plate, now I had to figure out if my idiot brother was on drugs. With a sigh, I trudged up the stairs.

I tried to come up with a plan of action. I had to be cool and casual. Lay some ground work, let him get comfortable and then maybe he would open up. Softly, I rapped on his door.

"Yeah!" He called out.

I pushed the door open and peeked inside. Little disclaimer here—I saw my brother almost every day of my life. However I very rarely paid attention to what he looked like. He's just Gabe. Right then, for the first time in I don't know how long, I really saw my brother.

"Holy crap, Gabe! You're friggin' huge!" My "play it cool" maneuver was off to a bang-up start.

63

"Thanks." He didn't tear his eyes off the television as he asked, "That all?"

Lounged on his black and tan striped comforter, he wore a raggedy, white t-shirt and a pair of navy blue, nylon-mesh shorts I had seen him in a thousand times. Only now they barely fit him. The shirt was stretched to its maximum capacity. His new bulging muscles strained against the thin material. If he sneezed, the shirt would be ripped to shreds. The muscles and veins in his legs protruded like the professional body builders in magazines. I could see the cause for concern now. This kind of change didn't happen naturally in a matter of days.

"No, I ... how did this happen?"

True to form, his sarcasm kicked in. "What can I say? I drank my milk and it did my body good. Now, go away." He turned the volume up on the TV to let me know we were done. I was nowhere near ready to give up.

I stomped over to the TV, clicked it off, and spun to face my brother with my hands firmly on my hips. "Are you on steroids?"

"What? No!" His face reddened as he scowled at my accusation. "How could you think that?"

"This," I gestured at his new mammoth frame "—is not natural! So, if it's not drugs, then you tell me what's going on. Tell me how you managed to look like a runner-up in a Tough Man contest in such a short amount of time."

He sprang off the bed and stalked over. His hot breath assaulted my face as he snorted down at me. I'm used to feeling small next to people; however, his increased muscle mass made me feel downright puny. He could snap me like a twig if he wanted to. With that in mind, I realized angering the heaving beast might not be the best idea. Self-preservation made me take a tentative step back. He matched my step and leaned down, his face only inches from mine. Every muscle in his body tensed. His hands balled into fists. His nostrils flared. I stared him down. Roid rage or not, I wasn't going to let him bully me.

Through his locked jaw he snarled, "I. Don't. Know. Maybe it's something in the Tennessee water. Or maybe I'm becoming the friggin' Hulk. I have no idea! But I am not on drugs. And the fact that you would even accuse me of that..."

"Look at the way you're acting," I said in a purposely calm voice. "Tell me this doesn't seem like stereotypical 'roid rage.'"

"This isn't 'roid rage.' This is annoying sister rage."

"What about your anger, like, twenty-four/seven? That my fault, too?"

He squinted at me in confusion but didn't deny it. "What makes you think I'm angry?"

I decided now wasn't the best time to mention my little talent. "Because I know you."

He gave a bitter laugh. "You know me, huh? Yet, you don't know that after everything that I've been through, I wouldn't touch drugs? And you can't think of any other reason in the world why I might be upset?"

"What do you mean?"

He leaned back and mulled over his words before he spat them out. "Like life has been so great I should be turning cartwheels?"

"What exactly is so terrible, Gabe? Moving here?"

"No."

"Then what? Are you ticked at Mom for sending us here?"

"No!" He turned on his heel and stalked to the window. With his arms folded tightly across his massive chest, he glared out into the darkness. "Mom's doing all that she can for what's left of our family."

A familiar cloak of sadness swept over me. I slumped down on my brother's bed, my hands folded in my lap. "Is this about Dad?"

Silence was my confirmation.

"How long have you felt this way?"

"Gee, Celeste, I don't know. How long has Dad been dead?"

"You've gotta let it go, Gabe. It was an accident. A terrible accident. We all miss him, but he'd want us to move on. To find a way to be happy again."

"See, that's where you're wrong." He pressed his forehead against the window pane.

"What? Of course Dad would want us to be happy."

"No, that it was an accident."

I choked on a shocked, humorless laugh. "He was hit by a car during a routine rescue. How can that be perceived as anything other than an accident?"

His anger reignited. He spun on me. "Because he didn't have to be there! He knew he had a family at home that needed him, but he didn't even stop to consider us before he strolled out into the street to save a guy that he didn't even know!"

I softened my voice to mask my brewing anger. "It was his job, Gabe. He was an EMT. What was he supposed to do? Let the guy die?"

"If he had, he'd still be alive. And I needed him here because I wasn't ready. I wasn't ready for any of this!" Gabe waved his arms in the air in a broad gesture.

"Any of what?"

"To be the man of the family! As soon as that title was given to me, look what I did. Look at how I screwed it up. I'm a failure because I wasn't ready. If Dad had just walked away..." Gabe's rant trailed off. He stared at the wall instead of me. His chestnut eyes glossed over with tears he was too proud to shed. I wanted to comfort him but didn't dare touch him. I knew he'd bristle at any act that threatened to expose his vulnerability in any way.

I twisted my hands in my lap as I sought out the right words. "If he had walked away, he wouldn't have been able to live with himself. That's just who he was."

"Because we weren't enough for him." Gabe rubbed his hand over his head and donned his best "unaffected-by-life" facial expression. His go-to façade to cover his pain. "He had to be the hero and get his name in the papers."

That was it. That was my limit. I felt bad for the pity party my

66

brother was enduring, but I wasn't going to let him rewrite history and paint our Dad as the villain. I stomped across the room toward my gigantic brother. At the sound of my heavy footfalls, he pivoted toward me. The sting of my unexpected slap snapped his head to the side and reddened his cheek.

Tears rimmed my eyes, and I was fairly certain I was snotting on myself, but I was too angry to care. "The only paper he got his name in was his obituary. He was doing his job. What happened was a freak accident. He wasn't thinking about leaving us behind. He was thinking about the man lying on that street and how much his family probably needed him." I turned to leave the room and then paused at the doorway. "So you made a mistake, Gabe. No one holds it against you. We don't think you're a failure. But we will if you don't grow a pair, get over it, and move on. Then maybe someday you'll be half the man Dad was, and you'll understand what it means to put other people first. Oh, and if you *are* doing steroids, knock it off. You're scaring Grams."

With that I slammed the door.

CHAPTER 11

After that little episode, Gabe's invitation to join me in the mountains had been revoked. And if he wasn't going, I saw no point in dragging Kendall along. I shoved supplies—a couple flashlights, bottled water, bug spray, matches, and a sweatshirt—into a backpack for a solo excursion. The feathered woman had answers. I was going to find her and learn how to stop the man-panther. Manther?

Heaven help me!

That's the only way to describe the emotion that jolted through me. My hands white-knuckle-gripped my backpack, and I doubled over as a swirling, tumultuous mess of emotions slammed into me. The heavy heart of deep seeded humiliation. The outstretched compassion of sympathy. Gnawing isolation. Gut wrenching pain. One by one they came at me with a speed and strength that took my breath away.

I didn't have to reach out for these. They pounded into me like waves against a rocky shore line. I couldn't stop them. Couldn't hold them back. But I knew who they were coming from. She was coming this way. Something had happened to Kendall. My trip into the mountains was coming too late.

I dashed across the room intending to track her down. It wasn't difficult. I swung open the bedroom door, and there she stood. I couldn't hold back a gasp at her ghostly, haunted appearance. Her normal peaches and cream complexion had turned stark white, her trembling lips a pale shade of blue. She stared past me with glassy, unseeing eyes.

Despite the door already being open, she extended her hand and turned a knob that only existed in her mind. She shuffled into the room, completely unaware of my presence. She bypassed both beds and the chair at our desk. Instead, she zombie-walked to the farthest corner of the room. With her back pressed up against our lilac-colored wall, she slid down and landed on the floor with a heavy thump.

"Kendall?"

"I—I—I—" Her mouth opened and shut, but she couldn't make it any further than that.

I squatted down next to her and stroked her soft hair. "You what?"

Slowly, her head turned toward me, her eyes wide and unblinking. "I flew."

As I had never heard a declaration like that before, all I could think to say was, "Huh?"

She shifted her gaze back to the wall. "Nothing beneath me but air."

The bird-woman's warning echoed in my mind. *"The changes will start now, Celeste. Not just for you, but for Gabe and Kendall as well."*

I shifted and sat on the floor next to my traumatized sister. With one arm around her slender shoulders, I drew her to me. When her head settled on my shoulder, I asked, "How did it happen?"

"Keith kissed me. My first kiss..."

"Your first kiss?" I interrupted. "Guys follow you around like puppy dogs."

"Just friends," she explained vacantly. "Keith's special."

Really? Sweaty, twitchy Keith? "Okay, you kissed. Then what?"

"He was the first to notice. He looked down and screamed. I didn't understand why. He pushed me away and fell. At first I thought we had somehow moved to the edge of the porch, and he'd stumbled off the edge. But then I looked down. I was floating." Her questioning eyes probed mine, looking for a logical explanation to this impossible scenario. "How is that possible, Celeste?"

"I don't know, Keni. I honestly don't."

"It only lasted for a second … then I came crashing down. Keith was petrified. He ran inside and locked the door behind him. He looked at me through the glass like … like I was a …"

"Freak?" Gabe's harsh interjection startled me. Not just because I hadn't heard him enter the room, but also because of the sharp way he spit the word out. Hostility brewed just below the surface, barely contained.

Kendall either missed the tone or ignored it. "Yeah, like a freak. I feel so bad for him. He was terrified. I don't know...what happened? How did I…?"

I hugged my baby sister tightly. If I hadn't been so slow to put the pieces together, Kendall wouldn't have had to endure this. This was my fault. "I'm so sorry," I muttered.

"You should be sorry," Gabe hissed, his voice pure venom.

I made no attempt to hide my exasperation as I shot back, "What is your problem, Gabe? Do you have something you wanna say?"

"You bet I do. Why don't you tell Kendall the truth? Or are you completely incapable of that anymore?"

"What exactly is it that you think I'm withholding?"

"That you know exactly what's going on," he snarled through gritted teeth. My heart momentarily forgot to beat. He knew. I didn't know how much. But judging by the way he was pacing, it was enough to make him fume. "I just figured it out. That's why you've been acting so weird lately. But instead of clueing us in on what was going on, you left us out to dry. Oh, but not before you took a minute to accuse me of doing drugs. Plenty of time for that fun little conversation." His body language dared me to challenge him.

My mouth fell open to say … what? I couldn't deny it. He was right. I hadn't even thought that his recent growth could be mystical, but it had to be. My chin fell to my chest. "I don't know much yet."

Kendall's head whipped back and forth between Gabe and me. "What are you guys talking about?"

"Kendall and I have turned into freaks. What about you? Are you a member of the freak brigade?"

"Wait! You can do weird stuff, too?" Kendall perked up at the idea that she wasn't the "lone freak."

"Yes. Try to keep up!" Gabe snapped.

I grabbed my sister's hand to comfort her, and then fixed my gaze on my pushy brother. "I can feel people's emotions, and I think I may be able to alter what they're feeling."

A smug smirk spread across Gabe's face. "Doesn't that put a fun twist on this story. You could even feel the confusion and stress we were going through as we…" he struggled to find the right word "…changed. Still, you said nothing."

I jumped up off the floor, stood on my tiptoes, and went nose to nose with my monstrous brother. "What did you want me to say, Gabe? That night I came home from the woods covered in blood, should I've told you that the real reason I fell was that I saw a feathered woman in the clearing? And that she told me stuff was going to start happening to all three of us. What do you think you would've said if I had done that?"

"You still could've given us a warning …"

"What would you have said?"

His mouth snapped shut. The fire in his eyes simmered down to embers. "I would've told you that you were crazy."

"Exactly. Truth be told, I thought I was. So I didn't feel inclined to announce it to the world. And just so you know, I just put all the pieces together tonight."

Gabe rubbed the back of his neck. Even a casual motion like that caused his giant pecks to dance. "I was just looking for someone to blame. Sorry. But, you can change how people feel? Really? That's kinda cool."

"*Hold on a second!*" Keni scrambled off the floor. "Feathered woman? Feeling people's emotions? What the heck is going on?"

Gabe's head jerked in Keni's direction. "Can't you use your voodoo to calm her down or something?"

"I'm not real sure how I did it the first time." I shrugged.

"I don't need to be calmed down!" Kendall stomped her foot. "What I need is for you two to tell me what is happening and why I am suddenly able to float!"

I didn't know how to explain it, especially when I really didn't understand myself. To the best of my ability, I started at the beginning and laid out the whole story of my experiences over the last week. I ended by declaring that to find answers we needed to find the bird-woman.

Gabe peeked into my backpack, taking inventory of what I'd packed. "It took you this long to figure all that out? Little slow on the uptake?"

"Definitely, yes."

"That's sad," he taunted. "So, we need to go back to that spot in the mountains and look for her. When do we go?"

"Tonight. After Grams crashes for the night. We'll head up to the clearing. Hopefully, she'll be there."

With resolute nods, we all agreed.

"Wait, I have a question." Kendall plopped down on her bed and grabbed her big stuffed zebra, Mr. Hoofington, that she'd had since she was four.

"Just one?"

"To start with." She looked up at Gabe as he zipped my backpack. "You didn't say what you could do."

"In addition to this..." He made a flippant gesture at his new, alarming frame. "I'm wicked strong."

"Cool." She picked a fuzzy off Mr. Hoofington and cocked her head to the side. "Wait. In addition to what?"

Now it was Gabe's turn to look puzzled. "What do you mean 'what'? This!" He extended his arms and pointed blatantly at himself.

Kendall sucked in a shocked breath. I bit down on my lip to stifle a laugh. "Holy crap, Gabe!" she exclaimed. "You're huge!"

"You both suck," he grumbled.

CHAPTER 12

Extended cab or not, all three of us crammed into the front seat of my truck. Uncertainty made togetherness mandatory. As we piled out into the deserted parking lot, I eyed the entrance to the path. It seemed more menacing at night. Billowing trees arched up over the entrance with a few ragged branches jutting down. It looked like a fanged mouth, like the hungry jaws of the mountain were eagerly awaiting the opportunity to swallow us whole. I wiped my suddenly sweaty palms on my blue jeans and moved a little closer to my brother and sister.

Gabe grabbed the backpack and pulled out both flashlights. He tossed one to Keni and the other to me. Of course I missed and mine went skittering to the ground. Keni clicked hers on to help me find mine, while Gabe tried to wrestle his gargantuan arms into the normal-sized backpack. Light retrieved, I watched the comic relief my brother was unknowingly providing a little longer than I should have before I had mercy and held out my hand for the bag.

He threw it to me and huffed. "Stupid, tiny bag."

Together we faced the mountain.

Keni shifted antsily on the balls of her feet. "I'm like, pee-my-pants scared right now."

"Aw, come on, Keni!" Gabe grinned as he draped his bulky arm around our little sister's shoulders. "It's a pitch-black mountain range, filled with savage, wild animals. One of which could be a man-eating panther. What's to be afraid of?"

Keni's eyes popped. Even in the moonlight, her complexion paled noticeably with dread.

I kept my voice as calm and soothing as possible. "Kendall, he's kidding."

Gabe released Keni and shoved her playfully toward me. "No, I'm not."

"Shut up," I hissed at him. I caught my sister's face in my hands and made her look me in the eye. "We'll be fine. And if we do run into any animals, Gabe is with us. So we have nothing to worry about."

Gabe expanded his chest in full meathead bravado. "That's right, ladies, the G-Man will protect you."

"Actually, I meant that any carnivorous animals would much rather eat you, in all your meatiness, than us." Gabe scowled. But I got a giggle out of Kendall.

She filled her lungs with a deep inhale and nodded. "All right. Let's go."

Gabe led the way with his wide gait and determined strides. I turned my head to hide my nervous gulp from my sister, then I followed him. Keni brought up the rear, sticking so close to me that she stepped on my heels repeatedly.

The foliage on the path hung thick and heavy and prevented the moonlight from poking through. Darkness enveloped us. I could only see as far as my flashlight beam allowed. Yet Gabe stayed out in front, sans flashlight.

"Hey, Gabe. Why don't you let someone with a flashlight lead?" *Or better yet, take the flashlight and let me stay safely in the middle of the pack.*

"That's all right. I don't need it. I can see fine."

I raised an eyebrow at that. Improved night vision too? And the freak traits just keep on comin'.

The nighttime hoots, calls, and screeches of the nocturnal forest animals were creeping me out enough that I was relieved when Keni piped up...at first. "Hey, Cee, with that ability of yours, can you read my mind?"

"No, it doesn't work that way."

"Quick! What color am I thinking of?"

"I have no idea; I'm not a mind reader. I'm empathic, not psychic."

"Do you, like, know what the winning lottery numbers are going to be?"

"Nope."

"Can you tell me if I'll get the role of Maggie the Cat?"

"I don't know the future, Keni. Sorry."

"Could you do something that would, like, completely alter what's going to happen in the future?"

I stopped and spun on her. "What? That doesn't even make sense! Anyone could do that. It's just about emotions, that's all."

With one hand on her hip and her interest in this matter obviously waning, she asked, "So, what am I feeling right now?"

I didn't even open the channel but went for the obvious. "Nervous and scared."

"Well, duh," she tsked. "Your ability's dumb. I can float."

I didn't mind the nighttime forest noises as much after that. Twenty minutes later, we arrived in the clearing. We were welcomed by the moonlight that glistened off the brook.

"You two have a seat over there." Gabe nodded in the direction of the fallen tree. "I'm gonna make a fire."

Keni and I watched him get a small campfire going. We gathered around it to fight off the night chill and watch for the bird-woman (I really hoped she had a name so I could stop calling her that).

"Hey, Gabe," Keni mused as she twirled an oak leaf between her fingers, "how'd you find out that you were super strong and not just big and lumpy?"

Gabe laughed and stretched his long legs out in front of him. With his back against the downed tree, he laced his fingers behind his head. "It was last week. I was on the bench press, lifting with the team during practice. No matter how much weight I slid on the bar it felt like nothing. I stacked more and more on until I ran out of weights. Still it didn't even challenge me. That's right about the time the steroid rumors started."

"Naturally," I commented.

"It got weirder from there." Gabe gazed into the fire, a smile tugging at his lips. "The guys on the team wanted to know how far back I could push the tackling dummy by myself with four guys standing on it."

"How far did you push it?" Kendall asked.

Gabe hesitated. "All the way down field, from end zone to end zone."

I called him on his loaded pause. "And..?"

"And more and more guys kept jumping on."

"Exactly how many were on it, Gabe?"

He tried to sound sheepish, but couldn't conceal his beaming, macho pride. "The entire team."

"*The entire team!*" Kendall and I chorused.

"Yep."

"Were they freaked out by it?" Kendall asked, ever the compassionate one.

"No," he snickered. "But I don't have to tell them things twice during practice anymore."

"Maybe we all play it a little bit more low key from now on," I suggested.

"Easy for you to say. You're used to living in the shadows." Gabe's statement was rude, but he had a point.

"Even so."

He shrugged off my words and turned to Kendall with a wry smile. "I have a question, Keni."

She eyed him warily. "What?"

"Keith was your first kiss. That right?"

"Yeah. Why?"

"You kissed a guy and then floated? Geez, can you imagine what would happen if you let him get a little boobage?" His eyes widened in mock alarm. "Lasers might shoot out of your eyeballs. You could completely eviscerate the guy."

Gabe let out a loud guffaw while Kendall spun on me. "Could that actually happen, Cee? Did your little birdie friend say anything about laser vision?"

I whipped a pine cone at my brother's head. "I didn't really talk to her as much as run screaming from her. But, no, she didn't mention laser vision. Ignore him."

Keni latched on to the sleeve of my sweatshirt. "With all the other strange stuff going on, it could happen! You can't say for one hundred percent sure that it won't!"

"No. You're right. I can't." I peeled her grip off my sleeve and patted her hand. "For the time being you should probably stick strictly to hand holding."

"Yeah, that's probably a good idea." She enthusiastically agreed.

I was internally patting myself on the back for simultaneously calming my sister down and talking her out of any ill-timed kanoodling when a light appeared from within the mass of trees in front of us. I sprang to my feet, my heart rate in overdrive.

"She's here."

Gabe and Kendall rose, and the three of us walked to the edge of the clearing. The illumination drew closer. We instinctively backed up. The vegetation in front of us parted and out she stepped. Six wide, unblinking eyes gaped at her. Her form had changed from the last time I saw her. She looked...angelic. Glowing ivory wings fanned out behind her. Her ankle length gown was comprised of golden feathers. Dainty white feet poked out from under it as she stepped onto the grass. The feathers on her head had been replaced by waist length, auburn waves that cascaded down her back. Her skin and features were that of a porcelain doll, yet the irises of her eyes were still the yellow of the eagle.

"You're beautiful." Gabe marveled and blushed bright red.

"Thank you." Her voice and grammar were practiced perfection. She extended one arm, sleeved to the wrist with flaxen feathers, to hand me my satchel that I had dropped at our first "encounter."

"I believe this belongs to you. Your drawing is quite good. I hope you are not bothered that I looked at it."

"No, it's cool," I squeaked. My hand shook as I accepted my satchel. "What...or, uh...who are you?"

"My name is Alaina. I am here to guide you."

"You know what's happening to us?" Gabe asked.

Alaina lowered her head in a regal nod. "I have the answers you seek. It is my job to prepare you for what is to come."

"And what is that?"

A dark shadow seeped into Alaina's avian eyes and creased her otherwise unblemished forehead. "War...against an evil man and the army he has created."

Gabe gave a flippant snort. "Lady, I hope you're packing an Uzi under those wings if you think we stand a chance against an entire army."

The smile she graced him with caused my big brother to omit an audible sigh. "When the time comes, you will have all you need to fight and to win."

I was cold, tired, confused, scared, overwhelmed, and I kind of had to pee. My patience was wearing thin. I crammed my hands into my pockets and tried to keep the snarkiness out of my voice as I asked, "How about a little less cryptic and a little more information?"

Those golden eyes locked on me. "You are absolutely right. Too much time has been wasted. It is time for each of you to embrace your destiny."

CHAPTER 13

To know what is to come, you must first know what has been."

Alaina pulled a small, black velvet drawstring sack out from within the folds of her feathered gown. Gabe, Kendall, and I were seated around the campfire while she stood. "That story takes us to the green, sprawling hills of Ireland in the 17th century—the bloodiest time in the history of Ireland. Civil wars tore the country apart and ended lives. An evil ex-soldier by the name of Barnabus chose to take advantage of the chaotic carnage by assembling his own army to challenge the governing power, the English Commonwealth. He was able to recruit roughly two dozen men, yet that was nowhere near enough to accomplish their goal."

She poured what looked like silver sand onto her palm and sprinkled it into the campfire in small, circular motions. The flames rose up in response, licking high up into the night sky. "They targeted small, insignificant villages, stormed tiny settlements, and demanded that the males of all ages join their army. When any man refused, he was forced to watch as his family was brutally killed. If men dared band together in refusal, their entire village was torched and the remaining residents slaughtered. Whispers of these massacres reached my own village." At the mention of her village, the silhouette of it appeared within the red and orange flames. Gabe, Kendall, and I leaned in and stared in astonishment at the small, plank-board-sided homes that could clearly be seen against the backdrop of the fire. "At word of the potential threat, our men made makeshift stands on the four corners of our town and kept watch at all hours. What happened next you need to see for yourself."

A loud trumpet blast came from the scene within the flames. Men, women, and children, all clad in sleepwear, scrambled out of the tiny homes.

"Cool! It's like a little movie," Kendall chirped.

I elbowed her in the ribs. "Shhh. Is that you?" I pointed to an auburn-haired girl of about fourteen that had stepped out from the most modest of the homes.

"It is," Alaina said sadly. The Alaina from the fire movie held a beautiful, cherub-faced boy of no more than six in her arms. A raven-haired woman stepped up behind her and hurried them both out of the house. "That is my brother and my mother."

Before I could ask what happened to them, a fully dressed man with a sheathed sword slung beneath his big ole Santa belly began to hush the townsfolk. He had a mass of curly, auburn hair that blended right into his bushy beard.

When the people quieted, he spoke in a thick Irish brogue. "There are roughly two hundred soldiers on horseback headed straight for us. They're armed with broad swords, axes, and arrows. The few weapons we have will be no match against their armor."

An old, grey-haired woman with a long braid down her back and a face that could scare children squeezed her way through the crowd. "What do we do? Can we run?"

"We'll ne'er get out of the gorge in time," the man beside her answered, shaking his head. "They have us cornered."

"Adara! Cadence!" the curly-haired man boomed. "Hitch four horses up to the wagon in my barn. Now! Move!"

Two young women in long, flowing nightgowns darted off. The man then walked over to young Alaina, squeezed her shoulder, and stroked the cheek of her brother.

Alaina answered the unspoken question. "My father."

His strong voice quaked as he laid out his plan. "We will load the children into the wagon and hold off the army so they can escape."

With somber resolve the villagers hitched up the horses and began their tearful goodbyes. Heartbroken parents loaded their sobbing and confused children into the wagon, unsure if they would ever see them again. The last child to be loaded was Alaina's own brother.

Tears streamed down his pink cheeks as he called out for his mama. His small hands clung to her clothing. Alaina had to pry his hands free and then held her mother tightly to prevent her from scooping him out of the wagon. Her mother collapsed on the ground wailing as the wagon pulled away.

A lone tear streaked down our Alaina's face. "That was the last time I saw my brother. Or any of the children for that matter."

"This is so awful!" Keni hiccupped and wiped her nose on her sleeve. "It's worse than watching *Titanic*!"

The village men grabbed their swords and positioned themselves at the edge of town as the echo of thundering hoofbeats drew near. The women clung to each other trembling and openly praying. Together they prayed for their loved ones to be spared. For the children to reach safety. For mercy. For...a miracle.

A flurry of chaotic activity erupted within the village. Fabric ripped. Women shrieked. A burst of feathers. Men crumbling to the ground. The roar of a lion, followed by another, and another.

"Uh...what the heck just happened?" Gabe asked.

"Just watch." Alaina's eyes were intently fixed on the scene.

The incoming horde of soldiers trembled in their metal boots when they saw what awaited them within the village—a pride of lions and a flock of winged women. In spite of their fear, the soldiers attacked. Arrows sliced through the air. One hit an ivory wing and bounced right off.

"That's the moment we figured out our feathers were impenetrable," Alaina commented. "We became the lions' shields."

Lions sprang at the soldiers, their monstrous paws knocking them from their horses. An elaborately armored soldier shouted to burn the village. He had to be Barnabus. Torches were cast onto the rooftops, setting the homes ablaze. Busy battling the army, the villagers could do nothing to prevent it. The younger Alaina snatched a soldier right off his horse, flew him high off the ground, and dropped him.

I looked up at Alaina. "Nice move."

She lived through the battle, but still couldn't tear her eyes off of it. "He did not die. At least not that day or by my hands."

Even with their new gifts, the villagers were losing ground. Dozens of soldiers would team up against one lion. They closed in on them in tight circles and blocked any protection the feathered women could offer. I squeezed my eyes shut as one of the mighty cats howled in pain, then crumpled to the ground in a bloody heap.

A deafening screech pierced through the night. My eyes snapped open. After a brief moment of panic, I realized the sound came from within the flames. Soldiers and villagers alike froze as a menacing-looking creature flew over the burning town and landed in the heart of the battle. His enormous wings arced up behind him as he glared down his beak at the soldiers. That pull I felt when I touched the statue in the garage returned with a vengeance. I leaned closer to the flames. I wanted to know every nuance and color change of his feathers, the consistency of his fur, the shade of his eyes, whether his scent was feline or avian, everything. However, unless I wanted to stick my head directly into the fire, these precise details would elude me.

Beside me, Keni crinkled her nose. "What the heck is that thing?"

Alaina opened her mouth to answer, but I beat her to it. "That's the Gryphon. The Protector of the Divine."

"He's a badass." I had to agree with Gabe as the Gryphon tossed soldiers around like ragdolls.

He towered over the soldiers' horses. As he stalked toward them the spooked equine reared up and bolted, whether their riders stayed on or not. With his help the villagers finally began to overpower the army. Some of the once indentured soldiers took advantage of a weaker Barnabus and turned on their captors with unexpected vigor.

Either a steel or feathered shield blocked every blow. The swipe of a flesh-shredding claw or the swing of a blade matched every attack. Some soldiers lost their lives while others surrendered and ran. When it became obvious he couldn't win, Barnabus ordered his troops to fall back. They gratefully obliged.

Barnabus himself hesitated before making his escape. He raised one armor clad arm in the air and pointed at the Gryphon. "This isn't over beast!" He then yanked his horse's head around and galloped off.

Except for the snaps and hisses of the burning homes, there was silence. All the villagers turned to the Gryphon. He stared off after Barnabus long after the evil man vanished into the night. Sorrow clouded his eyes. From the cluster of people, a young girl stepped forward. She looked about the same age as Kendall. Her slender frame seemed dwarfed by her long, mahogany locks and the new feathered appendages that fanned out behind her as she walked. The other villagers gaped at her courage as she approached the Gryphon and laid her delicate hand on his shoulder.

"Thank you for your aid. And for the gifts you bestowed on us." With a slight nod, she motioned to her wings. The Gryphon craned his head around to see her. She flinched, but didn't shy away. "May I ask what is troubling you in the wake of our victory?"

With a deep, resonate voice, the villagers' champion spoke. "I can feel the obsession that has formed in that man at the discovery of me. He will hunt me down. Of that, I am sure. A war will follow if I am to fulfill my destiny and protect my charges."

"And if he captures you?"

The Gryphon's feathers ruffled, then smoothed. "If the receptacles of divinity that I guard fall into his hands, the balance of good and evil would tip in favor of darkness."

She couldn't let him fight alone! Not after how he saved them!

As if my thoughts willed her into action, a look of steely determination overcame her dainty features. "You didn't let us stand alone, and I will not let you."

The Gryphon snapped his beak and shook his enormous head. "No. This war will rage on long after your mortal life has ended. I have foreseen it."

"Then my heirs shall take up the cause as well!" The girl lifted her soot-covered nightgown enough to allow herself the movement needed to go down on one knee. She stretched her wings out behind her and pressed her fist over her heart. "It is my pledge to you that the O'Garren family will join you in this crusade. My people will be your warriors until we find victory or death."

Goosebumps sprang up on my arms. I knew the name O'Garren. I had uncovered it during a genealogy project at school. A few generations later it had been changed to Garrett.

"The human spirit never ceases to amaze me. You, lass, are a shining example of that." The Gryphon swung his impressive frame around to face her full on. "My acceptance comes with strict conditions. The first is that I will only call upon your family if all other choices are exhausted. The next—I will choose only three. One will be the Protector, to shield against danger. One will be the Guardian, to fight with raw determination. The third will be my Conduit, the chosen mortal I will channel my powers through. Together they will be warriors on Earth."

The girl's hair fell in a curtain around her as she bowed her head in agreement.

The scene faded away, and the fire extinguished itself down to embers.

CHAPTER 14

Gabe prowled the length of the clearing in agitation. "So because of some stupid deal an ancestor of ours, about a million times removed made, we have to fight for this half-bird, half-cat thing?"

"To over simplify a complex matter, yes." Alaina said with a serene smile.

Gabe stopped in front of her and planted his feet. "Explain to me why this is our problem? I watched your little fire skit." He waved his arm at the still smoldering embers. "That Gryphon's a big, scary dude. Why does he need us to fight for him? Why can't he fend for himself?"

Alaina's smile vanished. Her head twitched to the side in a bird-like manner. "He is not allowed on this plane of existence. He should not have ventured here to save our town, yet he did. Believe me when I say there were repercussions for that above and beyond this matter with Barnabus. Yet he had hoped to eradicate this issue himself. Unfortunately, that was not to be.

Barnabus' obsession led him to seek help. He sought out a mysterious woman with a vast supply of mystical power. Very little is known about her, but we know she goes by the title of Countess. Rumor has it she once held regal stature until her ties to the dark arts were discovered. Children in her village went missing. It was believed she sacrificed them to unholy forces in exchange for greater powers. A torch and pitchfork-wielding horde chased her into exile where Barnabus found her. He told her of the Gryphon, and she agreed to help him. She ordered him to gather all his men and bring them to her. Their Dark Army assembled...then vanished."

"Vanished?" I gasped. I hadn't even noticed I'd been holding my breath.

With her hands behind her back, Alaina paced in front of us. "We believe the Countess took them all to the Underworld but cannot confirm this. Only demons, devils, and other malevolent beings can venture there. Since then, we have relied on the occasional informant to get whispers of what they are doing. This is how we learned of the impending attack."

"We?" Kendall asked, her arms wrapped tightly around herself.

"Yes, we. My family was massacred that terrible day. I begged the Gryphon to take me with him to the Spirit Plane. My heroism in my village qualified me for a position as a Spirit Guide, and here I am."

"Kudos on the promotions and all, but I don't understand why all this is happening now." Keni's voice was rapidly transitioning into a full out whine. "Centuries have passed! Why couldn't they attack sooner, like before we were born? Or better yet, why can't they just let it go?"

"In alternate dimensions such as the Underworld or the Spirit Plane, time passes differently. A rapid succession there takes centuries here. As sorry as I am to say, a battle is imminent."

A fire raged in my brother's eyes. "If it's the Gryphon that Barnabus wants, then I say let him have him! Give me one good reason why I shouldn't just walk away?"

Alaina crossed to Gabe. She didn't shy away but met his gaze with passionate resolution. "You have been chosen and that cannot be undone. You can accept that and prepare yourself, or you can sit idly by and wait for them to find and kill you. Your powers will emerge and once they do, they will draw the Dark Army to you like a lighthouse beacon. The choice is yours."

"Uh, that's not much of a choice," Kendall squeaked.

"And you really believe we can take down an entire army?" A hard lump of disbelief seemed to be lodged in my throat.

She didn't hesitate for a second. "If you let me train you, you can."

Gabe, Kendall, and I looked from one to the other and back again. Kendall nodded. I nodded. Gabe groaned. "All right. Arm us with knowledge."

"As I explained three are chosen: the Protector, the Guardian, and the Conduit. The Protector is the essence of the eagle." Another bird-like twitch as Alaina looked to Kendall. "She will take the same form the women of my village did—a winged heroine. The Protector is a creature of love that uses their flight, impenetrable wings, and healing feathers to protect those they love."

"I'm going to grow wings and fly?"

"It appears that is your calling, yes."

Keni twirled a lock of hair around her finger. "Hmm…I'm going to have to seriously reconsider my wardrobe options."

Alaina seemed uncertain of how to respond to that. She opted to ignore it and move on to Gabe. "The Guardian, the sentry to the Conduit, takes the form of the lion. Their brute strength and raw, feline instincts make them a formidable adversary to any that means to harm their charges."

"I'm going to turn into a big, hairy lion?" Gabe jammed his hands into the pockets of his jeans. One corner of his mouth pulled back in a smirk. "That's actually kinda cool."

"So that means Celeste is the...what did you call it?" Kendall asked.

Alaina's avian eyes zeroed in on me. "She is the Conduit."

I shifted uncomfortably. "What does that mean? What's gonna happen to me?"

Her shoulders and wings shrugged simultaneously. "That I do not know."

"What?" Everyone else knew exactly what was in store for them. It seemed cruel and unfair that she couldn't offer me that same courtesy.

"Don't you live with the Gryphon? Didn't he clue you in on his plans for me before he booted your butt to earth?"

She held up one finger to correct me. "I live on the Spirit Plane where the Gryphon resides, but we are not roommates. And I do not know what it means for you because you will only be given talents and abilities as the need arises. Your circumstances will decide your path, and that I cannot predict."

"Crappy excuse for a guide you are," I grumbled.

"Have you not yet received any talents?"

"You know I have. I'm an empathe. You left me a nifty little note about it, remember?"

"Note?"

"Yeah." I reached into the backpack and pulled out the note I had thrown in on a whim. I handed it to Alaina and watched her eagle eyes flick across the scroll as she read.

Her brows lowered. Her lips set in a firm line. "I did not give this to you. I have no answers as to who did. But...you can read this?"

"Of course I can read it. Why wouldn't I be able to?"

Kendall jumped up and strode to Alaina. She peaked over her shoulder at my note. "Oh, yeah, that's not English."

I scrambled to my feet. "What? Of course it is!"

Alaina handed me the paper. "The empathe feels the emotions of others. This power is meant to guide by 'listening' to those in need of aid." I read out-loud. "Seriously, are you guys messing with me?"

"Celeste." Alaina's tone was patient, if slightly bewildered. "That is written in Gaelic."

"No it's not," I argued and checked the scroll again.

"An Bhfuil Gaeilige agat on will gale-geh ah-gut?"

"Gesundheit."

She looked at me like she wanted to tie me to a table and do experiments on me. "Fascinating. You cannot speak the language, but you can read it."

I threw my hands in the air in frustration. "Well, what the heck does that mean? And who left me this note?"

"It means someone else is attempting to guide and influence you." Alaina's delicate jaw tightened as she spoke. "As we do not know who it is or what their motives are, this is a matter of great worry."

I held the parchment between two fingers and eyed it like it was a snake about to strike. "Someone that may want me dead left a note on my pillow? Fantastic. Anyway we can tell the Gryphon about this, so he can zap me a method to protect myself?"

Alaina folded her hands in front of her. "He already knows. He keeps an ongoing link with your thoughts, so he is aware of any situation that may require his attention. When he knows you are in need, he will grant you the power."

The Gryphon was in my head? The "Protector of the Divine" rummaged around in my thoughts whenever he felt like it? I tried to think back to where my mind may have wandered since my bump on the cranium. No doubt there had been some unsavory stuff in there.

Alaina noticed the sweat that broke out across my forehead and my pained expression. She took my hand in hers. Her touch was unbelievably soft, like the whisper of a feather being dragged over my skin.

"Celeste, he only uses your thoughts and experiences to be his eyes and ears here on earth. He does not pry any further than that or pass any judgments."

"But...but...I'm eighteen! Teenagers...as a rule...think dirty stuff!" The hyperventilation portion of my panic attack approached right on schedule.

With an exasperated sigh, Gabe grabbed the back of my neck and shoved my head between my knees. "Breathe, you dope."

"Is she okay?" Kendall tried to brush my hair back off my face. I swatted her hands away. "She turned kind of grey."

"She's fine. She just needs to grow a pair and deal with it." Gabe joyfully reveled in the opportunity to throw my own words back at me.

Kendall scooted closer and bent down to peek at me from under my knee. She spoke in a confidential whisper. "If you have some sort of sick or kinky thoughts that you're worried about, maybe you should just tell Alaina. It might make you feel better to get it out."

That brought me around quick. I flipped my head up and glared at my sister, who wore the sincere expression of someone who thought they were helping. "*I do not have any sick or kinky thoughts!*"

Gabe snorted his disbelief.

"Oh, like your mind is squeaky clean!"

"Never said it was." Gabe shrugged. "I'm a twenty-year-old guy. If the Gryphon was in my head, he'd probably feel the need to shower often, if you know what I'm sayin'."

"You're disgusting," Kendall grimaced.

"Yeah, he's gross. But he's making my point for me!"

Alaina intervened as the voice of reason. "Celeste, the Gryphon is an imperfect being that makes mistakes just like everyone else. In my village, he took lives. Human lives. He knows what he has done. He will pass no judgments on you. You have nothing to worry about."

"Fine." I huffed. "But I am *not* okay with this."

"Noted. Now, can we get back to the legion of killers heading this way?"

"Sure, go ahead."

"Somehow the Dark Army learned of our plans to call on you." Alaina resumed pacing. "However, they have not figured in the earthly time difference. It was a decade ago that … things … were put into motion to commence in choosing a Conduit. Yet they do not realize that and are looking for a child around eight or nine years of age."

I don't like being the center of attention. More than that, I don't like having a big, red bulls-eye painted on my back. "Uh, why are they looking for me at all?"

Alaina paused and looked at me as if I should already know that answer. "Because you are the Chosen One. You alone are linked to the Gryphon. If you die, he will be weakened. He cloaks the portal to the Spirit Plane. In his weakened state, he would not be able to maintain that glamour, and the Dark Army would gain entry. If that happens, if we cannot stop them, darkness will gain dominion over the earth."

"My death could lead to the end of the world?"

"Yes."

I looked longingly at Gabe and Kendall. "Does anybody want to switch callings?" To my dismay, they both shook their heads.

Alaina continued on as if she hadn't heard me try to pawn my sacred calling off on someone else. "The demons enlisted to track you down are called Seekers. They had been searching in Michigan but seem to have followed you here."

"The break-ins."

"What was that?"

"The reason our mom sent us here." Gabe sat down on the fallen tree trunk and scooped a handful of rocks off the ground. One by one he tossed them into our makeshift fire-pit. The set of his jaw and the tensed tendons in his neck hinted to the stress and agitation that still gnawed at him. "Houses in our neighborhood kept getting broken into. Nothing was ever taken, but the places were trashed. It must have been the Seekers looking for her. How will we know these guys if we see them?"

"The Seeker that is here in Gainesboro is a shape-shifter that can transform into a..."

"Panther," I finished for her. "That's why he was nosing around Ella. He's checking out kids about the right age. We have to stop him before he does something crazy like randomly killing kids in hopes of stumbling onto the right one."

Alaina drew her wings in close to her back, which gave her a more human appearance. "No, he may threaten, but he cannot risk killing the Conduit. Barnabus wants to dispose of it himself."

"Could you not refer to me as an 'it'?"

"Apologies," Alaina said with a formal bow of her head. "You must understand though that if a Seeker figures out who you are, it will notify Barnabus. Therefore, if the opportunity presents itself, you must not hesitate. It very much is a kill or be killed situation."

"*Wait!*" Kendall shrieked and hopped up off the ground. "We have to actually kill him? What if he's not evil at all? What if he just fell into this like we did? We can't destroy a life without giving the guy a chance to change!"

Gabe leaned back and supported his weight on his palms. Condescension dripped from his tone. "You wanna try to reason with the demon, Keni? Maybe get him into an evil rehab group? Then maybe he could get a job as a candy striper at a local hospital and devote his life to helping others. What do you think?"

Fury clouded Kendall's normally perfect face. She pounced at Gabe, and slapped at any part of him he didn't shield from her frantic blows. "*I am a creature of love, dammit! Did you miss that part? I don't want to hurt anyone!*"

Gabe risked a look up in between blows, "You sure about that?" he asked with a victorious grin.

Keni backed off and straightened her clothing. I glanced over at Alaina to see how she felt about this show of sibling love. With one eyebrow raised, she muttered under her breath, "Kids have changed over the centuries."

Awkward moment over, Gabe bounced off the log and clapped his hands in completely manufactured exuberance. "All right! We have absolutely no choice in this matter at all. It's do or die, and I—for one—don't wanna die. So, let's get our abilities up and running. Where do we start?"

"I appreciate your enthusiasm." Alaina totally missed his sarcasm. "For now, I am going to send the three of you home to get a good night's rest. You are no good to me exhausted. First thing tomorrow, we awaken your inner warriors."

CHAPTER 15

My thoughts turned dark as we headed back to the truck. It made sense for the Gryphon to make me his Conduit. I was his last resort. His panic button if Gabe and Kendall failed. But they wouldn't fail. They never did. They would embrace their new talents and keep me out of harm's way. I would remain an awkward, useless lump that they were now saddled with the burden of protecting. What kind of lives could they have if they constantly had to watch out for me?

I threw the keys to Gabe. I probably shouldn't trust myself to drive the *real* warriors around.

Kendall climbed into the back seat and laid down. In seconds her rhythmic snoring filled the truck. I clicked on my seat belt, then stared out the window at the outline of the mountain range.

"You know why he picked you, right?" Gabe asked.

"I have some idea," I mumbled.

"I bet you do." He pulled us out of the parking lot onto the road that led into town. "Want to hear my theory?"

"Not really."

"Tough. It's because you're the strongest."

97

"*Ha!*" I spat. "Yeah, 'cause I was the one that pushed an entire football team 100 yards."

"I don't mean physically. The physical strength he can give you. That's easy. But the spirit to fight had to already be there. Like it is with you."

"The spirit to fight? Look at me. I'm no fighter. There are elementary school kids bigger than me. And I'm pretty sure I wouldn't even win in a fight against them. Some of them bite."

"Are you capable of shutting up?" He snapped. "I'm talking about your spirit. Who you are, not what you are. You don't give up. That's just not you. When Dad died you made me get back into sports. You made Kendall go back to dance and cheerleading and every other thing she's involved in. You got Mom out of bed each day during the worst of it. You put everything on hold to get us back on our feet. We were all ready to curl up and die, but you wouldn't let us. You're the real fighter. Maybe you just became the Gryphon's Conduit, but you've been the power in our family for a long time."

That was the nicest thing anyone had ever said to me. I blinked back the tears that welled up in my eyes. "Thanks."

He grunted. His quota for sentimental conversation had been reached.

CHAPTER 16

I couldn't understand why I had to accompany Kendall for her first day of training. If the Gryphon was just gonna download stuff into my brain Matrix style it seemed he could do that just as easily if I was home on the couch. Plus, Gabe had gotten an excused absence because of a football scrimmage. So, why the heck did I have to be there? But it's next to impossible to debate things like this with a centuries old Spirit Guide. She used big words, rambled on about the fate of the world, duty and honor, until I gave in just to shut her up.

I was still hoping for a distraction to get me out of going, which is why I rushed to the door when a knock rattled it on its hinges. When I glanced out, I didn't immediately recognize the guy standing on our porch.

"What? Is my fly unzipped?" Alec smirked and made a big production out of double checking.

I made a concentrated effort to close my slack jaw. Turns out a great hair-cut and a fitted suit can do wonders. Alec had transitioned from boy-next-door cute to smokin' hottie.

"So?" he asked. He held out the lapels of his jacket and did a little turn. "What do you think?"

"You look..." *Awesome. Hot. Dreamy.* "...different."

"Good different or bad different?"

"Good," I sighed, then blushed beet red. "What brought this on?"

"That's kind of what I came to talk to you about. I owe you an apology."

"For what?"

"My behavior when I finally got you to go out with me. I let myself get really wrapped up in my story, and I think I came off as kind of a..."

"Jerk?"

"Yeah," he cringed. "Sorry about that."

"You don't owe me any apologies," I reassured him. "It's okay. You were just excited." With the whirlwind craziness I had been going through, Alec hadn't been top on my mind. He sure didn't owe me anything.

"Yes! Exactly!" His enthusiasm had him beaming. "I was excited because I realized what I'm supposed to do."

"What's that?" I giggled.

"I'm not supposed to be a cameraman. I need to be out there..." he waved his arm toward the outside world, "...finding the stories that need to be told and reporting on them. I talked to my producer at the station, and he made me a full-time field reporter. Apparently, he gave me this story in the first place because he thinks I have what it takes."

"And you do." I fought to keep the resentment out of my voice.

What a cruel joke for the universe to play—spruce him up to make him irresistible, then give him the job as a story chaser. And here I was sitting on the mother of all stories. A career maker, one that could get him killed if he snooped into it. With a heavy heart, I realized for his own protection I had to keep my distance from him. At least until the threats surrounding me subsided. My tension seemed to evade him.

"I went over to my mom's salon and made her day by letting her cut my hair. Then I visited a tailor and had some suits made that I'm hoping to be able to pay off someday. Now I'm all set to embrace who I was meant to be."

"There seems to be a lot of that going around lately," I muttered.

"What?"

"Nothing. I'm really happy for you, Alec."

"Thanks, but I really am sorry about the other night. You mean a lot to me, Celeste, and I would never want to hurt you." His voice grew husky as he moved closer. Warning sirens blared in my head. He had that "I'm going to kiss her" look in his eyes. He brushed the back of his hand down my arm. "I really would like to give us a chance."

I didn't give myself time to consider if I wanted to kiss him or not. (For the record—I did). There was a psycho shape-shifter out there terrorizing children. I didn't have time to play kissy face. Concentrating on my own reluctance, I brought my hand up to his cheek. With that seemingly loving gesture, I passed my hesitation on to him.

His face froze inches from mine. I could feel his warm breath on my skin and fought my desire to close the gap between us. His eyes clouded over in confused hesitation. From his shirt pocket, his cell phone buzzed.

"You should probably get that," I whispered.

His brow furrowed in uncertainty as he nodded and snatched his phone from its resting place. I backed away from him until I bumped into the wall. Temptation averted, he flipped open his phone. "Hey, what's up? The panther? Where?" My pulse quickened at the mention of the cat I knew to be a demon in disguise. "Oh, man! Is it still there? Awesome! I'm on my way!"

He snapped his phone shut and looked up at me like a kid on Christmas morning. "You are not going to believe this! The panther is on the roof of the grocery store. The fire department, the cops, and animal rescue are all there. They're going to try to shoot it with a tranquilizer gun to get it down. I gotta go!"

Before I could stop him, he grabbed me, spun me around, and dipped me back in a kiss straight out of *Gone with the Wind*. Then he stood me up, said "Call ya later" and ran out the door.

With the back of my hand pressed to my mouth, I stared after him, dumbstruck. I wanted so badly for him to come back and kiss me again, but knew that didn't coincide with my plan to keep my distance. My head and heart were battling it out when Kendall came pounding down the stairs.

"Do we have company?"

"It was Alec." I licked my lips. They still tasted like him. "He just left."

"Oh." She made no attempt to hide her disappointment.

I glanced over my shoulder at her. "You'll hear from Keith, Keni. I'm sure of it."

She gave a crestfallen shrug.

"Right now though, we have way more important things to worry about."

"What's up?"

"For some moronic reason, the Seeker is currently on top of the local supermarket creating a huge spectacle. Cops and everything. Apparently being evil also means you have the IQ of a zipper. We need to go awaken your inner eagle and lure him away from town, stat."

"And what do we do if he actually shows up?" A fair share of panic crept into her voice.

"I guess you better learn to fly quick so you can get us the heck out of there, huh?"

CHAPTER 17

Come to find out the first step in channeling one's inner eagle is meditation. I do not have an inner eagle. Therefore it made no sense for me to be cross-legged on the ground focused on my breathing. Concentration on anything wasn't coming easily. There was a Seeker in town doing God knows what—and my pants were soaked from sitting on the ground. I opened one eye and peeked at my sister. She was doing exactly as Alaina told her: eyes closed, head up, breathing deeply. If she was uncomfortable, it didn't show. Maybe the ground wasn't wet where she was sitting. If that was the case, I was probably sitting where some wild animal had recently...Eeew.

"Celeste!"

I sheepishly opened both eyes and peered at Alaina. With her hands on her hips and her cross expression, she was the picture of disapproval.

"Sorry."

"Will you please try to focus?" she pleaded.

"I'm trying. I am," I lied.

Again she began her instructions. "Close your eyes." I did.

"Now, inhale a deep, cleansing breath. Feel your lungs expanding to their fullest capacity. Exhale and blow out all the tension in your body. Good. Again, inhale."

I wonder what Alec is doing right now?

"All the stress is leaving your body, leaving you refreshed and rejuvenated. Inhale. Exhale. Your body is relaxed and your mind is free to roam."

And roam it shall …

"Let your subconscious focus on all those you love. Let your mind center on them. Open yourself to the love in your heart. Feel the warmth of it radiating through you. It's spreading through your chest, castings its glow through each part of your body that it touches. It reaches your arms and legs, right down to the tips of your fingers and toes."

Blah, blah, blah. For a Spirit Guide, she's surprisingly long-winded.

"Up into your head, even your hair is tingling. Every inch of your body is alive with the love that you possess. Let your entire being become encompassed in that beautiful feeling."

I wonder if Kendall is faking. She totally could be. I opened myself up to her to check. Love emanated off her with such a force that it made warmth explode through me. I had never felt anything like this. It was an amazing, euphoric high.

I could also feel that she was teetering on the precipice of her change. She was so close, but seemed stuck, needing a nudge to push her over the threshold. I centered everything I was feeling, drew it into a tight circle in my chest, and with a touch of my hand gave it to her. The energy passed through me and into her. She jerked at my touch and then absorbed the weight of what I'd given her like a person being electrocuted. She convulsed from head to toe. Her eyes rolled back in her head. A foamy, gurgled scream tore from her throat.

Panicked, I scrambled to get to my feet to aid my baby sister. Alaina intercepted me and physically blocked me from getting any closer.

"No," she whispered in my ear. "It's happening."

The trembling stopped. Keni sat ramrod straight, still as the dead. Her eyes popped open and stared straight ahead. Fabric tore. Alaina took my hand and guided me around to Kendall's side.

"You're going to want to see this."

I crinkled my nose. "I'm fairly certain I don't."

Two mounds of flesh rose up out of Kendall's shoulder blades. Slow and steady they grew. Thick stalks of cartilage drew outward to pull and manipulate the fleshy lumps into a taunt wing form. The bare flesh stretched out wide behind her. Fuzzy white down sprouted up to cover it. A beat later the down fell away to reveal silky, ivory feathers beneath it. Her wings shook and flapped off the remaining fuzz, then snapped open to exhibit the finished product. A gigantic pair of magnificent ivory wings protruded from my baby sister's back.

"Well there's something you don't see every day," I gaped.

"I do," Alaina corrected.

Kendall blinked rapidly as she regained the ability to focus. "What happened?"

I pointed. "Uhhh...those happened."

She glanced over her shoulder. "*Oh*! Whoa!!"

"This is great, Kendall," Alaina assured her. "This is exactly what we wanted to happen."

I'll admit my next little barrage of questions probably didn't help the situation. "What does it feel like? Do they hurt? Can you move them? Can I touch one?"

"No, you cannot touch one! Oh, this feels so weird! Like I just grew another set of arms or something," she groaned.

I couldn't stop myself from reaching out and rubbing one of her new feathers between my thumb and forefinger. They were soft, just like bird down. She jerked her wing away from my touch which sent her on a whole new tirade.

"Oh! It's moving! I'm moving it. I can move it, and it feels soooo gross!" She flapped her wings back and forth. "You have no idea how wrong this feels. I don't know how I'm doing it! Oh, oohhhh...this is so very, very, very, very weird! Uhhh!"

Alaina cradled Kendall's face in her hands. "Kendall, I need you to calm down so I can help you. Okay?"

"Slap her or something," I suggested.

"I am not going to slap her because she is going to calm down. Right, Kendall?"

My sister's wings did another involuntary flap. Even with her mouth clamped firmly shut, a muffled whimper escaped. Her eyes pleaded with our guide to somehow, someway, make this better.

"I need you to listen. The only way you are going to put your mind at ease is to learn to control them. Do you understand?" Alaina asked in her soothing made-for-radio voice.

"Mmm-hmm," Kendall squeaked.

"I want you to pull your wings in. It is an act similar to drawing your arms in to your sides. It will come naturally. You just need to try. Can you do that for me?"

"Nnn-mm." Kendall shook her head from side to side.

"Why not?"

Kendall's beseeching eyes met mine. I opened myself up to her, then answered for her. "It scares the crap out of her when she feels them move."

"I see. I suppose I should have explained myself better," Alaina said and stroked Kendall's cheek. "I am trying to show you how to put your wings away so that you can have a break from them."

Kendall's eyes widened with her desire to be rid of her new attributes for a while.

"Now can you give it a try?" Alaina attempted again.

Kendall's face turned stone serious. Her wings twitched inward and prompted another unintentional yelp. She set her jaw and tried again. In one rapid motion, like folding up an umbrella, they flattened together and disappeared into her back.

"There now," Alaina smiled. "Just an ordinary girl again."

A new realization dawned on Kendall, the fashion plate. "Hey! My brand new shirt is ripped."

"The sacrifices of being a superhero," I said sarcastically.

"I'll say. I loved this shirt. What the heck am I supposed to do, wear tank tops all the time?"

Alaina and I exchanged amused glances.

"How do you feel now, aside from your ruined garment?" Alaina asked.

"Better," Keni nodded.

Alaina offered Keni a hand to help her up. "I do remember that the first time is quite...disturbing. I promise you it does get easier."

"I sure hope so." Keni stood up and brushed off the back of her striped board shorts.

"You could prove it to yourself right now. Go ahead and expand them again."

Kendall hesitated for a moment and then closed her eyes. As if it was already a reflex, the awesome wings sprung open.

Her face brightened. "It was easier that time! Why was the first time so painful?"

With a bird-like twitch, Alaina cocked her head to the side. "It was painful?"

"Very."

I sheepishly raised my hand. "I ... think that was my fault."

Kendall scoffed. "Wings ripped their way out of my back and you think it's your fault it hurt?"

"I helped," I croaked.

Both the beautiful, winged women turned to face me.

"What did you do, Cee?"

"Meditating wasn't working for me. I wondered if it was working for you. So I felt your emotions, which were really nice. You were all glowy. But then I felt you get stuck, right before the change. So I channeled everything I was feeling. The good, the bad, the indifferent ... and I gave it to you. Sorry. So sorry." I rambled it all out, not even stopping to breathe.

Alaina gave me a maternal frown. "I was having her meditate on love because that is the emotion that triggers her change. Adding foreign emotions added pain." I gulped and prepared to be reprimanded. "However, you do seem to have mastered the skill to pass your feelings to others, so some good came from this."

"Was that a 'yay me'?" I asked.

"I'm pretty sure that was a 'next time keep your emoting to yourself,'" Kendall said and crossed her arms over her chest.

"Will do," I agreed. "Once again, so sorry."

Keni shrugged; her wings bobbed up and down. "Whatevs. So Alaina, when do I get to, like, fly and stuff?"

"Right now, if you are ready." To me Alaina added, "Would you please act as our look out while she practices? Keep a vigilant eye out for the panther. If he appears, warn us immediately. We will need to get you out of here at once."

I was used to fading into the background while one of my siblings shined in the spotlight, but it never bothered me as much as it did right then. I moseyed over to a nearby rock and sat down. Inadequate seemed too weak a word to describe how I felt as Kendall flitted up to the treetops. She was the embodiment of angelic beauty. Silken feathers framed her while her blonde hair cascaded around her shoulders. Based on sheer principle alone, this was cosmically unjust.

***

Sprawled out in our bedroom, Keni and I filled Gabe in on what he missed. More accurately, I tried to fill him in while Keni gushed over what it felt like to fly.

"...the wind was in my face. I could see, like, the entire mountain range. It was amazing."

"No you couldn't," I snapped. "Alaina didn't let you go above the tree tops."

"Well, you wouldn't know, being down on the ground and all, but from where I was, I could totally see everything." She rolled onto her back on her bed and made Mr. Hoofington "fly" over her head.

"Did the Seeker make an appearance at all?" Gabe asked while giving me a "does she have a mute button" look.

"If he was anywhere around, I totally would have seen him. Did I mention I could see everything up there?"

"It came up," I snapped and squeezed the pillow in my lap a little tighter. "He didn't show. Hopefully, it wasn't because he was busy feasting on express-line customers."

Gabe threw himself on my bed. The bed springs screamed as his enormous frame landed. "I doubt there was any bloodshed. Small town like this, we would've heard about it the second it happened."

I feared he would break the frame and swatted him off my bed. He groaned, but settled onto the floor. "True. Plus, Kendall just became a big neon sign pointing him to us. He won't waste his time in town much longer."

A knock on the door, then Grams poked her head in. "Gang's all here, huh? What are we talking about?"

"The panther in town," I answered truthfully. "Did you hear anything about what happened today?"

Fired up for a good bit of gossiping, Grams threw open the door with gusto. "Yes! It was really somethin'! They had that critter cornered up there on the roof. Animal rescue shot it with three different tranquilizer darts before it finally went down. Or at least they thought they hit the panther ..." She paused for dramatic effect. "But when they got up on the roof—no panther. There was a man up there that somehow got caught in the crossfire. No one knows who he is or what he was doing there. All they know is he was in the worst possible place at the worst possible time and got himself darted in the rump for it. They carted him off to the hospital in Nashville. Hopefully when he wakes up, they'll get some answers. Poor fella. Scared by a panther and then shot in the butt. That's a bad day, right there."

If all evil creatures are this incompetent, this saving the world thing might not be too tough.

"Wow...just wow," Gabe marveled.

"Excitement like that is even better than my stories!" Grams gushed and waved her freshly polished fuchsia nails in the air. "Anywho, I came up here to let ya'll know I'm off to Casino Night at the Bingo Hall. Gonna try my hand at Blackjack. Grams needs a new pair of shoes! Ha! You kids have a good night."

She planted bright red lipstick marks on each of our foreheads before she disappeared down the stairs. We waited until we heard the front door click shut behind her before we resumed our "other" identities.

"Am I the only one that expected more from the Dark Army than some spaz that gets darted by the local law enforcement?" I asked.

"Maybe he's new to being evil." My sister shrugged, then struck yet another Superman pose and giggled to herself.

"This may've bought us some time though. If he was unconscious, he probably missed Kendall's powers being activated." I ran my finger along the ridges of the Gryphon statuette on my nightstand and wished he could answer our questions directly.

"That's good. That gives us more time to prepare." Gabe seemed lost in his own thoughts as he stared out the door. "But what if they come here? What do we do about Grams?"

We all fell silent. The idea of Grams being harmed was unfathomable.

"She's never left alone," I declared.

Kendall and Gabe nodded in agreement. If the Dark Army wanted to come for us, let them come. But hands off the Grams.

CHAPTER 18

N o way. Unh-uh. I'm not doing that."

"What do you mean 'no way'?"

"I mean I'm not doing it, and you're not big enough to make me." Gabe folded his arms and scowled like an overgrown three-year-old.

Under her breath Alaina muttered, "I have powers, boy. I could make you dance like a puppet if I wanted to."

She must've forgotten his cat-like hearing. "Bring it on 'cause I'm not doing it any other way. I started gaining all this muscle mass while I was training with the team. Being active. Not sitting on my butt, chanting."

Alaina closed her eyes and sighed. Her wings sagged from her frustration. "You could have made that point first. What exactly did you have in mind?"

"Uh … I don't know." By the way he stammered he obviously hadn't thought that far ahead. "I could go for a run or something."

Alaina's auburn waves bounced as she shook her head. "That will not work. We have to awaken the lion. That is why I suggested the meditation; you could find the emotional connection to it.

111

Running will not have the same impact."

"Well, I'm not doing it," Gabe huffed.

"I have an idea." I squeezed the bridge of my nose, having passed the point of annoyance at their bickering about twenty minutes ago. "Why don't we smack him on the nose with a rolled up newspaper? See how his inner cat feels about that."

"Let's call that Plan B." He glared and then nodded in the direction of Kendall. "Hey, I could spar with Tweety."

Keni was completely unaware of our conversation. Alaina had her practicing take offs and landings. Judging by the way she spun three times in a pike position and landed gracefully on her tip toes, I'd say she was getting the hang of it. With a satisfied grin, she spun toward us, noticed we were all staring at her, and froze.

"What?"

"It could actually work." Alaina rubbed her chin with the tip of her finger as she mulled it over. "It is the nature of the beast to stalk and attack."

"Whoa!" I positioned myself between Gabe and Kendall. If he had to go through me to get to her, so be it. "Think about this, Gabe. If your plan works, our little sister is going to be up against a lion. Are you okay with that? 'Cause I'm not!"

Gabe grabbed me by my upper-arms, lifted me off my feet, and set me down out of his way. "She can *fly*, Cee! I'd have to catch her first."

"You must also remember that her wings are impenetrable. She would be in no real danger," Alaina tried to reassure me. It didn't work.

"Hello? Over here! You guys are obviously talking about me. Wanna clue me in?" Kendall marched over with her hands on her hips and her enormous wings arced up behind her.

Gabe's eyes flashed. "You get to help me activate my powers."

"How?" she asked, her unease evident.

"Gabe wants you to spar with him to help bring the lion out."

She cocked her head and gazed at me with narrowed eyes.

112

"You realize I don't actually have the brain of a bird, right?"

"Come on, Keni!" Gabe groaned and threw his hands up. "I'm not going to hurt you. Even if I do turn, it's still me. Right?" He addressed that last part to Alaina.

"For the most part, yes." Her tight-lipped smile made me wonder if she was being entirely truthful. "There are animal instincts you will have to learn to control, but it should not be a problem."

"Plus you have the 'force field' feathers, remember?" Gabe prodded.

Kendall's shoulders and wings slumped. "Fine. But if you bite me, and I have to get stitches, you're explaining it to Grams."

"Agreed," Gabe said with a wide grin.

As they walked to the center of the clearing, I was once again assigned the role of lookout. Bitterness oozed off of me as I plopped down on what was fast becoming "my rock." Gabe and Kendall each assumed their fight positions; he struck a standard wrestling stance while she stood ramrod straight with her wings curled in protectively around her.

"Ready to get your feathers plucked, Keni?" He swayed side to side as he prepared to attack.

"Noo!" she whined.

Ready or not, Gabe charged. He dropped his shoulder, fully intending to plow our dainty sister right over. I covered my eyes. Kendall squealed. There was a loud thud; something scooted across the ground, followed by a "*hhuuuufffff!*"

I peeked between my fingers. Gabe was sprawled in the dirt, flat on his back. As he pulled himself up, he let out a sharp laugh. It may have been my imagination, but it sounded a bit like a snarl. Immediately ready for round two, he crouched down. A fire building behind his eyes. He rushed her. Her wing shot up. This time Gabe expected it. He ducked under it and lunged for her legs. With one forceful flap Kendall lifted off the ground and out of reach. Gabe couldn't stop his momentum and tumbled to the ground—again. He got up, brushed himself off and backed away. With the wave of his hand, he invited her to land.

Her feet no sooner touched the ground, than Gabe launched at her again. He jumped up and tried to dive over her wing. It didn't go well. Keni canopied both wings over her head like any umbrella. He hit her impassable, feathered fortress head first. Dazed, he flopped to the ground. I hid my laughter behind my hand. Gabe had to shake it off and regain his bearings before he could stand up. Kendall gave me an uneasy look. I grinned and threw her two thumbs up.

Try as he might, Gabe couldn't engage Kendall in the fight. She could dance her way out of anything he threw at her. The lion had yet to make an appearance, but Gabe's irritation had.

"Come on, Kendall! You're all defense, no offense! You want to try actually being in the fight?" He growled as he kicked up a cloud of dirt and pebbles. "If I wanted no challenge at all, I would've fought Celeste!"

"Hey!"

"No offense, Cee." I wouldn't have taken offense had he not rolled his eyes when he said that. "But this is pointless. I'm not getting anywhere."

Alaina stepped forward from the perimeter of the clearing. "I was afraid of this. As a creature of love, she will not attack her own brother. Perhaps I can come up with something else for us to try tomorrow. I think I will venture into the Spirit Plane in search of other ideas."

I hopped to my feet. "Wait! You can just go back and forth between the two worlds?"

"Yes." Alaina rolled her shoulders and released her wings.

"When you go there, you can talk to the Gryphon?"

"Yes."

"Maybe on this little trip you'll tell him that I'm ready, and he can go ahead and upload some super strength into me. What do ya think?" I asked eagerly.

Her face fell. "I am very sorry, Celeste. However, that is something he just will not do. The truth is, he very much hopes he will not have to give you any powers."

Those words sliced into my heart like a knife. "Why? He doesn't think I could handle it?"

"No. That is not it at all." She laid a comforting hand on my shoulder. "I had hoped to prolong this conversation for as long as possible, yet it seems your inquisitive nature will not allow that. It is not known what it will mean for your human life if these powers are bestowed on you. To live as the lion or the eagle can be done. It can be suppressed and managed to make a normal life possible. However, you are the very first Conduit of the Gryphon. We fear that the more power is channeled through you, the less human you will become."

"Being human hasn't been a barrel of laughs so far," I grumbled. "I'd be okay giving that up."

A shadow of pain made Alaina's golden eyes fill with tears. "Things have been very hard for all of you. I understand that. But please keep in mind that there are beautiful experiences in this world. Experiences that only humans are fortunate enough to embark on. Do not be so eager to turn your back on them."

I was a horrible person. She had given up everything to become our guide in a moment when she felt she had no other options. And here I was rubbing salt in her wound. I made a weak apology.

She blinked rapidly and forced a smile. "Just try not to be so eager, Celeste."

I nodded. "Okay."

"You three head home. I will research our situation." As soon as the last word left her mouth, she morphed into the eagle and blazed off into the horizon.

"Wow." Gabe's eyes widened in mock awe. "You must really feel like crap right now."

"Yes. Yes I do. Can we go now, please?" As much as I wished he would leave this alone, I knew he wouldn't.

"Sure." A smile played at the corners of his lips as he motioned for me to lead the way. We made it all of fifteen paces before he started in. "I mean, you just made an angel cry. I can't say for sure that you'll go to Hell for that kind of thing, but it doesn't look good."

"Shut up, Gabe. And she's not really an angel."

"Keep telling yourself that. I'm sure you'll find it very reassuring while you're burning in the eternal Hell fires, right next to the puppy kickers."

I muttered a few expletives under my breath but kept walking.

Gabe matched me stride for stride. "I gotta ask, Cee, is it out of your system now? Or do you need to track down good ole Saint Nick and kick him in the crotch?"

"Leave her alone, Gabe," Kendall said as she trailed us. "She's got a lot on her mind right now!"

"Thank you, Kendall."

"Yeah. She's busy trying to find the Easter Bunny, so she can rip his fuzzy, little tail off."

I glared over my shoulder at her. "Et tu, Brute'?"

Their tittering laughter echoed through the forest.

I thought I had gained a good distance on them when Gabe jumped in front of me. With his back to me, he kept his gaze locked to the north of us.

"What now? Oh, ha, ha, ha. Is the Gryphon coming to settle the score for me making his BFF cry?" I tried to push past him, but he blocked the way with one enormous arm.

A hand locked onto my shoulder and pulled me back. I turned. Kendall silently motioned me to come to her. A low, rumbling growl escaped from my brother's chest. All the hair on the back of my neck stood at attention.

"What is it?" I whispered.

"We're not alone." Gabe's voice came out a deep, disturbing rumble.

"The panther?" Kendall asked, her tone surprisingly calm.

Another menacing growl confirmed it.

"We've got to go! We aren't ready yet for him to report us to Barnabus!" I grabbed Gabe's arm and tried to yank him toward the parking lot.

Gabe's head snapped around. To my astonishment, yellow slit cat eyes bore down on me. "Do you think you can outrun a panther?" he snarled.

I'm kind of worried about outrunning you right now.

Instinct made me release his arm. Despite my trembling voice, I tried to reason with him. "Gabe, you're getting ready to change. That's pretty obvious. If he sees that, he's gonna know. I am asking you, please, calm down and come with us. Now!"

The tall weeds beside us rustled. We were out of time. Gabe growled. His lip curled up to reveal sharp fangs emerging from his top and bottom jaw. Whatever was in the grass halted.

"Kendall, take Celeste and go," he rumbled.

I started to object. To demand that he come too. Then I caught sight of his skin. It rippled as if something crawled beneath it. Stretching. Churning. Preparing. As revolting as it was, I couldn't look away. Gabe hit a crouch just as the black panther slunk out from the reeds. As soon as it saw Gabe, its ears went flat to its head. It snarled and showed its teeth.

A mighty "king of the jungle" roar tore out of Gabe and shook the ground we stood on. The panther flinched. Its feline eyes widened. Its ears perked. No mere human could make that noise. Gabe just gave us away. With a roll of his neck, the panther turned his yellow eyes to Kendall and me. Did you know panthers can smile? They can. It's terrifying.

Gabe entered the next, more gruesome, part of his transformation. Beneath his seemingly elastic skin, his skeletal system began to shift. With sickening snaps and pops, his bones dislocated, then reconnected in their new formation. Hair sprouted up on him, everywhere. As awful as it was, my masochistic eyes refused to look away.

Gabe's head swiveled to Kendall and me, as the bones in his face separated and locked outward to form a wide muzzle. "Rrrrrun, dammit!" he yelled in a barely human tremor.

That was it. It was time to go. I grabbed Keni's arm and scrambled down the path. Roars, lashes, and snarls quickened our pace as the two cats collided in battle. True to form, I tripped and went face first into the dirt. Air whooshed behind me as Kendall freed her wings. She hooked me under the arms, and we went airborne. Careening at top speed, we made it back to the parking lot in no time. A distressed yelp resounded from the direction of the ferocious felines. There was no way to know if it was our lion or the Seeker in trouble.

Kendall retracted her wings, and we continued on foot. My whole body quaked as I fumbled to get my keys out of my pocket. I succeeded in the difficult mission of unlocking the doors, and we dove inside, slamming the locks down behind us.

I started the truck—then waited.

"We're not leaving without Gabe. But this way we can take off as soon as he gets here," I said to reassure myself as much, if not more than, my sister.

She looked at me with tears filling her eyes, her hand still gripping the door handle. "Did you hear that cry? What if Gabe can't make it out?"

That was an option I couldn't consider. "He'll make it."

CHAPTER 19

Seconds ticked by. We didn't move. Didn't blink. Just stared at the entrance to the path. There was no sign of movement. Panic churned my stomach. I couldn't leave without my brother. If I had to go look for him, that's what I would do. My hand trembled as I reached over and unlocked my door. The sound of its release whipped Kendall's head around.

"What are you doing?!"

"He may need help. I'm going to go find him. Stay here and lock the doors. If anything bad happens, you just go. Got it?"

"I can fly and you can't. There's no way you're leaving me here. If anything you should stay behind." She unlocked her door to further punctuate her point.

"Fine. We'll both go."

I stifled my own fears and opened the door. When a gigantic jungle cat didn't leap out at me and rip my head off, I hastily climbed out. On the other side of the truck, Keni did the same. Afraid to make too much noise, we quietly clicked the doors shut behind us. I dragged my feet forward and met my sister on the passenger side of the truck.

We had taken no more than five steps toward the path, walking shoulder to shoulder, when a loud thud behind us made the ground shudder under our feet. Keni and I clung to each other as we spun around. There, taking up the entire bed of my S-10, stood an enormous lion, licking its chops hungrily. I heard a whimper that I was fairly certain came from me. The mighty beast's muzzle twitched, and a low rumble leaked out.

"That's Gabe, right?" Kendall whispered with urgency.

"Uh-huh."

In one fluid motion, the enormous cat leapt to the ground. Kendall and I squealed and clung to each other. He stalked around us, every step punctuated by a snarl. Not wanting to have our backs to him, we shuffled in a circle right along with him.

"If that's Gabe, what the heck is his problem?"

"I'm going to go out on a limb and say that his 'problem' is that he just turned into a friggin' lion!" I cried.

Gabe lurched forward and swiped at us with his massive paw. The threat of his bone shredding claws sent Keni and I screaming and scurrying up onto the hood of my truck. He paced back and forth in front of us, occasionally darting in for another swipe.

"Alaina said he wouldn't have any problems!"

"She said he would have to learn to control his lion instincts!" I corrected as I pulled my legs up under me. Gabe lashed out again. "*Aahh!* And apparently that's the issue right now!"

"Gabe?" Kendall tried to sound calm despite her shaky voice. "You need to, like, fight this, okay? You're stronger than this. So just overcome the lion, or whatever!"

He bellowed out a thunderous roar and slammed his shoulder against the side of the truck. The collision nearly dumped us to the ground.

"If you dented my truck, you're paying to fix it, Fluffy!" Gabe's argument to the contrary was to viciously swipe at my arm. His claws came so close I could feel air whoosh over my bare skin. I felt it was a valid point.

"What are you doing?" Kendall hissed. "Don't yell at him!"

"Got it!" I squeaked.

"Can't you throw an 'I don't want to eat my sisters' emotion at him!?"

"That's a human emotion! He's a lion! I don't think that's going to help us right now!" I squirmed up my windshield and onto the roof, which dented in under my weight. "Dammit! My truck!"

"Would you please just try? Instead of waiting here for him to kill us?" she begged.

"Fine. It couldn't hurt." Gabe lunged at the truck again. His jaws snapped itches from my foot. "But that could," I whimpered.

Kendall scooted up next to me and cocooned us both in her wings. Cautiously, I reached out for Gabe's emotions. I was prepared for hunger, bloodlust, or some other form of gruesomeness. What I found was amusement. I cocked my head, and narrowed my eyes at the humongous cat. If he really wanted to, he could've jumped up here and made dinner out of us. But he hadn't. There was a very good reason for that.

In a huff, I climbed down off my truck. "Gabe Allen Garrett, you suck!"

"What are you doing?!" Kendall huddled under her wings and shielded her eyes from what she assumed would be a tragic bloodbath.

"He's messing with us, Kendall."

With the jig up, Gabe sat down on his haunches. His eyes crinkled as his mouth fell open in a menacing, jagged-toothed grin.

Kendall peeked over her wing and made the international sound of annoyed teenagers everywhere. "Tsk-uhh."

"So where's the Seeker, Mufasa?" I asked with my hands on my hips.

Gabe turned his nose up and snorted scornfully in the direction of his altercation. Thinking he had bought us some time, I approached the newly formed Gabe-lion. His appearance was staggering. Even seated, he was taller than me. His head was bigger than a beach ball. The dark, chocolate-colored mane that haloed it was the same color as Gabe's hair. Somehow that eased my nerves. It showed a visible connection between my brother and the carnivorous cat.

"What does it feel like Gabe? Is it scary?" Kendall asked as she climbed off the truck.

Gabe sprang to his feet and used his entire body to emit a potent, "ROOOWWWWWRRR!"

"I think that means he likes it," I laughed.

Suddenly, the lion's head whipped to the tree line. He growled as he slunk over to my truck. He looked at me and slammed his paw against the door.

"Easy!" I snapped. I walked over and opened the door for him. "I'm not kidding, Gabe. You mess up my truck and you *will* fix it."

He crinkled his muzzle and snarled.

I snarled back.

He sniffed at my pathetic attempt to be intimidating and then dipped his head down to the floorboard where his duffle bag sat.

"What's that?" Kendall asked.

He pivoted and held the bag toward me so I could unzip it. "He brought other clothes," I answered for him. "I take it yours didn't survive the transformation?"

His shook his head then trotted off into the woods with the bag held in his teeth.

"Wish I would have thought of that," Kendall said wistfully. "I really liked that shirt."

I gave her my best sympathetic face, forced as it was. "I know you did, sis. I know."

A moment later, human Gabe jogged out of the trees, his face a stern mask. "We gotta go. I thought I chased the panther away, but I can smell him moving this way. If we don't want him to follow us home, we need to get some distance now."

Kendall's nose crinkled. "Smell him? Gross."

"Be grossed out later. Right now, be mobile."

We piled into the truck and sped off toward home. I glanced in the rearview mirror as I steered us out of the parking lot. A chill ran down my spine. From within the shadowed foliage, a pair of yellow cat eyes stared back at me.

CHAPTER 20

My tires screeched as I whipped into Grams' driveway. The sun hung low in the sky. Before the truck came to a complete stop, Gabe flew out the door.

"I'll check around back," he called as he raced around the side of the house.

Kendall and I jumped out, then scanned the street to make sure we weren't followed. If a battle was going to take place, we didn't want it to happen here. Here there were innocent bystanders, like our much adored Grams, that could get hurt. Regret gnawed at me. We shouldn't have doubted ourselves. We should've stayed in the mountains and squared off with the Seeker. Our hesitation may have endangered lives.

Gabe rounded the house in an easy jog. "There's nothing back there. I can't sense him anywhere nearby. I think we're okay for now."

"Sense him?" I asked. "Is that another cat thing?"

He wiped the sweat from his forehead. I guessed it was from the muggy night and not the exertion from the run because he wasn't even winded. "It's like a prickly feeling at the back of my neck, telling me there's another predator around. Plus I can hear and smell him miles away. The panther won't be able to sneak up on us now that I've changed."

"As long as he comes in panther form." I pulled my hair up off my damp neck.

"What?"

"He can shape shift, remember? The lion will detect the panther but not a human."

Gabe thought on that so hard it looked physically painful for him. "We need to find him before he finds us. First thing tomorrow I'm gonna go up into the mountains and try to draw him to me. Then, I'll take care of this once and for all."

"Once and for all?" Kendall cringed.

"Yes, Kendall. I will kill him," he stated firmly. "Because if I don't, an entire army is going to show up on our doorstep wanting Celeste's head on a platter. I personally would like to avoid that, wouldn't you?"

Keni emphasized her agreement with a series of vigorous nods.

"I'm also a fan of avoiding the whole head on a platter thing," I offered. "Especially with it being my head in question."

"As for tonight," Gabe's eyes were shaded by his heavy brow as he peered at the house. "We'll take turns as look-out. That way we can each get some sleep. When I go tomorrow, you two sit tight here. Keep each other and Grams safe. I'll handle the panther. Should be a piece of cake. The guy can't be too tough if he got darted in the butt."

His cavalier attitude would've been more believable if we didn't have axes of death and mayhem dangling over our heads. But there was no point in arguing. "Sounds like a plan."

"Good. I'll take first shift. Keni, you get second. You'll be last, Cee."

Big shocker, I got the last shift—sunrise. The least likely time for an attack. My own insignificance in the face of adversity ground into me like a dull knife. However, at that moment emotional pain wasn't exclusive to me. Across the street, Keith dragged garbage cans out of his parents' garage and down the driveway. Kendall's turquoise eyes brightened, and her cheeks flushed to a rosy hue.

"Keith!" She took a couple of eager steps toward him.

Her crush glanced up, then quickly lowered his gaze and stared at the ground for the duration of his task.

"Keith?"

He disappeared back inside without acknowledging her at all.

Kendall's chin quivered. I wrapped my arm around her and stroked her hair the way I'd seen Mom do a thousand times.

Leave it to Gabe—a.k.a. Mr. Insensitive—to take the tough love approach. "Get your head in the game, Keni. After we save the world, you can worry about that mushy stuff."

She blinked back tears and managed a nod. My heart broke for her.

"Let's call it a night, guys." I jerked my head in the direction of the house. I didn't have to tap into her emotions to know Keni needed a little girl talk.

Halfway up Grams' meticulously landscaped walkway, I halted. Despite the heat, I got an unmistakable chill. We were being watched. I rubbed at the goose bumps that had popped up on my arms and glanced around into the impending darkness. I saw nothing but couldn't shake that foreboding feeling.

CHAPTER 21

K endall and I stoically watched as Gabe prepared for his trip into the mountains. I had to purposely avoid the thought that he might not come back in one piece, or at all.

In an uncharacteristic display of affection, he kissed both Keni and me on the forehead. "Stay here, and stay together. I'll check in as soon as I can."

Part of me wished he could leave in lion form. Seeing a vicious beast skulk off to face danger would've been easier than watching my big brother leave. One saving grace in all this was the golden eagle that circled the skies over Gabe's head. Alaina would watch his back. I let out a slow breath as gratitude filled me.

Putting on airs of normalcy for Grams wouldn't be a problem. She took herself out of the equation—and scarred us for life— when she came out of her bedroom in a leopard print bikini on her way to the community pool. Apparently they hired a new lifeguard and Grams had yet to determine if he was "eye candy" or not. It seemed Gabe wasn't the only one on the prowl today.

With her out of the way, Kendall and I were free to worry ourselves into a tizzy. We straightened up the entire house in an attempt to distract ourselves. It didn't work. Suffering the maddening wait prompted me to take preventative measures. I sat on the porch, closed my eyes, and tried to channel Gabe. If I could feel his emotions, I would know he was okay. I just needed to concentrate.

"Whatcha doin'?" Keni asked as she plopped down in the rocking chair beside me.

"Trying to get a read on Gabe."

"Good idea! What's happening? Has he found him yet?"

"I don't know, Keni. I have to be able to focus."

"So focus already. What's the hold up?"

I opened my eyes and stared at her.

Keni flipped her hair and huffed. "Oh. Well, I don't need conditions to be perfect to use *my* power, but whatever. Focus away." I rolled my eyes and tried again to channel him. I had just found Gabe's essence and was about to open myself up to it..."Tsk, I broke a nail. It must've been when I sparred with Gabe. Craptastic."

The severity of this situation was lost on Kendall.

"Why don't you go inside and find a nail file?" I suggested through clenched teeth. "I'll let you know as soon as I find out anything."

She narrowed her eyes. "Are you trying to get rid of me?"

"Yes."

"At least you're honest," she said with a lift of her shoulder, and she hopped up to go in the house.

Finally, I was able to get a lock on Gabe. The lion hungered for the kill. I found it comforting to be connected to him. It assured me he was safe. I stayed with him as he caught a whiff of another animal that made his carnivorous stomach grumble. I sensed his disappointment that it wasn't the victim he longed for. Time passed. The lion hunted. His tension grew with every moment the panther failed to appear.

"He's getting frustrated," I murmured to myself.

"Why would he be frustrated?" Keni's voice made me jump in my seat. I'd been so focused I didn't know she'd come back out.

"My best guess is that the panther isn't taking the bait."

"Which means he could be anywhere." Keni had been leaning up against the porch railing. In one graceful motion, she windmill kicked her long legs over the rail, then dashed off to do a quick scan of the area.

"Don't show your wings unless you have to," I called after her. "We don't want to scare the neighbors."

"Go in the house and lock the door until I get back!" I wasn't used to taking orders from my little sister. Yet seeing as she had invincible feathers and I didn't, it seemed like as good a time as any to start.

Back in the house, I didn't know what to do with myself. The Seeker could be anywhere. He could be watching me right now...

Fear shivered through me. I snatched the remote from its resting place on the coffee table and clicked on the TV. I didn't care in the slightest what was on but needed the noise to distract and sooth me. My fidgety hand clicked the channel up button incessantly.

Flip.

Flip.

Flip.

Flip.

Flip.

A pair of menacing cat eyes on the screen caught my attention. I stopped and backed up to the program. It was a documentary on the hunting style of predatory cats. A lion stalked a herd of wildebeests.

"The fierce predator singles out the weakest member of the herd," the narrator explained. "In this case, the baby."

The remote slide from my hand and clattered to the floor. The baby. Kendall!

I raced for the door and flung it open. There stood Kendall in an unperturbed, unruffled state.

"All clear. Whoa! Okay." I grabbed her in a tight bear hug. "Everything ok, Cee? I was only gone for a minute."

"Yep. Just had myself a nice little panic attack."

"Planning on letting go of me any time soon?"

"Nope. Gonna be a minute." I squeezed her and took a few deep breaths. When my heart rate dropped and the ringing in ears stopped, I released her from my death grip. "Sorry."

"Quite all right." She laughed and handed me a stack of envelopes. "Here, I got the mail. Now I need a drink of water. It's like a hundred and fifty degrees out there."

I followed her into the kitchen, flipping through the mail as I walked. Somewhere in the middle of the stack was a plain, white envelope with "Kendall" scratched onto it. There was no return address or stamp. Someone hand delivered it to our mailbox. Fearing it might explode or release some terrible parasite, I dangled it between two fingers.

"Recognize the handwriting?" I asked.

Her forehead creased and her wings instinctively popped out, knocking over a dining room chair. "No."

With her indestructible wings curled around her, she took it from me and tore it open. Inside was a lone piece of notebook paper. No big *kaboom* or scary white powder.

Whatever was written on the paper brought a new light to her face. Her wings retracted and her eyes sparkled. "It's from Keith!"

I expelled a sigh of relief. "What does it say?"

"He wants to see me tonight at the library. He says we have a lot to talk about and he hopes I'll meet him there at six. Oooh, and he misses me." She hugged the note to her chest.

I hated to be the bad guy, mostly because it meant I would have to listen to her whine, but I didn't have a choice. "Keni, in the entire history of mankind, that is absolutely the worst idea ever. The Seeker could be anywhere. We have to stick together. You're going to have to reschedule for a night when our lives aren't in peril."

"I can't!" she moaned. "If I blow him off tonight, he might not give me another chance! And with this new superhero thing, our lives are always going to be in peril! I *have* to go, Celeste! Pleeeeeeeeeezzzzzzzzzz!"

Trying to reason logic against fifteen-year-old hormones—a losing battle if ever there was one. "What if you run into the Seeker while you're with Keith? Do you actually want to risk him getting hurt?"

"No, of course not. But we could make a deal," she bargained. "You could keep spying on Gabe's emotions. When you feel him get a lock on the panther and know everything is, like, all clear and stuff, I can go. If not, I'll stay put."

I hated to make any kind of agreement with her; however, this did give me a workable excuse to use. "Okay, but if I can't get a definite read off of Gabe, you stay here without any whining. Deal?"

"Deal!" She gave me a quick squeeze then skipped across the kitchen toward the stairs.

"Where are you going?"

"I have to decide what to wear, duh!"

"Yeah, there won't be any whining at all when I tell her no. Right," I grumbled to myself as she disappeared up the stairs.

I had no intention of letting her step foot out of the house. But the girl could fly. There was only so much I could do to physically keep her here. My options were screaming, chasing after her, or dangling off her as she flew. My maturity must be a work in progress because I didn't consider any of those things beneath me.

To placate her and check in on the status of things, I went back outside to channel Gabe. His frustration remained the same. Just like before, I stayed locked on to him until the afternoon sun began to hang its weary head. The dusky sky meant six o'clock must be drawing near. The unpleasantness of telling Kendall "no" wasn't far off. Yippee.

Out of the blue, a jolt of adrenaline shot through me. Gabe was on the chase and after blood. He closed in for the kill. I could feel his desire to sink his teeth into the tender...

Ok, gross. Quickly, I shut myself off from the Gabe-lion. Whatever he was about to do was going to be messy, gory, and gruesome. I really didn't want to experience that with him.

As if cued, Kendall danced out the front door. Up on point, she twirled an arabesque, her violet sundress fanning out around her. She ended in a deep curtsy, then flashed me her best angelic smile. "So, can I go?"

"He's in pursuit right now. But he hasn't caught him yet. In no way is this even remotely close to settled." I hoped her better judgment would finally show itself. No such luck.

"He's as good as caught!" Kendall relaxed her posture. "And we know right where the Seeker is now. So there's no reason I can't go. I'll make it quick and be back before you even know I'm gone. Please, Celeste? I really will hurry back. I promise!"

She folded her hands to beg and pleaded with her eyes.

As inopportune as her timing was, she did have a point. We knew right where the Seeker was. Gabe had him engaged in a bloody, toothy battle. If that changed, I would know. I could get down the street and around the corner to her quicker than the panther could get within threat range. As much as I hated to admit it, a short visit probably couldn't hurt.

"You have half an hour," I stated. "After that, I won't hesitate to find you and drag you home by your stupid, perfect hair. Understood?"

"You're the best, Cee!" she gushed then flitted down the stairs and pranced toward town.

With her gone, I did my best to relax. I got myself a glass of sweet tea and returned to the porch to watch the sunset. I thought the picturesque scene would help calm my frazzled nerves. It failed tragically. As soon as I lost sight of Keni, I began to rethink my decision to let her go. I had put too much confidence in my new, untested, and therefore unreliable, ability. I glanced through the screen door at the wall clock inside. She had been gone for ten minutes. I would be true to my word. She had twenty minutes left, then I was going after her. I gazed back at the beautiful pink, purple, and gold shades that decorated the horizon and hoped for the best.

It occurred to me that there was a simple solution to calm my tension. The icky parts between Gabe and the Seeker were most likely over. I just needed to tune back in. Once I felt Gabe's sense of satisfaction, I would know it was safe and everything was okay. I closed my eyes and sought him out. What I found instead was deep disappointment and revisited frustration.

Wait, what does that mean?

I frantically calculated situations in my head that would lead him to those emotions. Only one made sense. The Seeker had gotten away. Panic shoved its way in, and I desperately tried to keep it at bay.

That doesn't mean Kendall's in danger. I internally reasoned. *Gabe saw the Seeker in the mountains. You have time. Get a grip, so you can calmly go get her.*

As I rose to do just that, the game drastically changed. I heard a door creak open and instinctively glanced up. My breath caught in my throat. Keith moseyed casually from his house to the garage. The same Keith that was supposed to be at the library with Kendall right then. My legs were already in motion while my brain tried to put the pieces together. I made it across the street in a flash and roughly grabbed the scrawny boy by his forearms.

"What are you doing here?" I demanded.

"I ... I live here," he stammered, his eyes as big as saucers.

"You told Kendall to meet you at the library!" I screamed, terrified because I suspected what his response would be.

"No ... I ... I didn't."

Releasing the frightened boy, I spun and ran with every ounce

of strength in my body.
"Is she okay?" He yelled after me.
No, she's not. And it's my fault.

CHAPTER 22

My bare feet slapping against the blistering blacktop made each step more excruciating than the last. My lungs ached and I had a stitch in my side, yet I ran on. I had to.

As I sprinted into town, I opened up my direct line to Gabe. I shoved my panicked, urgent feelings out to him. *Please, please let him get here in time,* I pleaded to the heavens.

My foot found a pothole on Gore Avenue, and my ankle wrenched to the side. I caught myself with my hands as I fell. My ankle throbbed and my palms were bloody. I righted myself as quickly as I could and hobbled on.

The library came into view, spurring me to limp-run even faster. My eyes scoured the yellow building for a glimpse of her. No movement, no people, nothing. They couldn't be inside, the library closed at five.

Evil, malignant beings don't really care about closing times or locked doors, my inner voice corrected. *If he wanted in, he got in.*

I yanked and shook the doors with all my might. They were

padlocked with a thick, steel chain and determined not to budge. I cupped my hands around my eyes and looked inside. I saw nothing but books. If he took her somewhere else, I had no way to find her.

Or do I?

My chest tightened. Opening myself up to that, knowing there was nothing I could do to help her, would be agony. But I had to find her. I braced myself for the worst and reached out for her.

Like a cold, hard fist ramming into my chest and squeezing my heart, her feelings came to me. She was terrified, fully believing that she was about to die. Tears sprang to my eyes and streaked down my cheeks.

Try to concentrate. Where is she? I closed my eyes and focused.

My head snapped back as her location revealed itself to me. They were three stories up on the roof, and the door in front of me was locked. I darted around the building, desperately searching for another way in. Finding a back door, I grasped the handle and shook. Nothing. No time to lose, I kept moving. I continued around the building, trying every door and window for some way to gain entry. I wound up back where I started, with nothing to show for my efforts.

I glanced around frantically hoping to see Gabe or a three story ladder. Neither of those things magically appeared. There was nothing I could do to help her. I would be willing to trade my life for hers if I could just get to her. But I couldn't. I reached out for Gabe, feeling a strong, steady confidence from him. He felt certain he would make it in time. A blood-curdling scream from above argued otherwise.

"*Kendall!*" I shrieked. "Gabe's coming! Just hold on!" I doubted she heard me, but I had to try.

Her scream became a choked gurgle—then silence. I hunched forward, my fingernails digging into my face. I had to do something. In seconds, it would be too late.

"*In a manner of speaking, he can read your mind.*" My psyche provided Alaina's words when I needed them most. The Gryphon knew what I was thinking! Boy, did I have an earful for him.

I know you can hear me, so listen up. You picked me to help you and to risk my life against all odds. But if Kendall dies, the deal is broken. I don't care what my ancestors vowed to you, I make my own destiny. I will not lift a finger for you if you don't help me keep my family safe. Do you hear me? Do you understand? If she dies, it's YOUR fault and I AM OUT!

I don't know what it looked like when it happened. There were no witnesses that could later regale me with tales of my transformation. I do know what it felt like. If a rogue storm cloud had invaded the clear night sky and threw one bolt of lightning straight at me, the feeling would've been comparable. An intense, jarring energy jolted through my system. Every muscle in my body went rigid with the surge. My head flew back. My arms and legs locked straight out. I trembled and quaked; my stomach rolled at the intensity of it. Then I fell to the ground in a heap.

I stayed slumped on the ground, deliberating over whether I was dead or not. It seemed dead would hurt, and I had no pain. As a matter of fact, I had never felt more alive. Sitting up, I gazed down at my hands and forearms. I turned them over and back again. They looked exactly the same. There was no outward sign of change. Yet, everything was different. The power was there, just below the surface. I could feel it.

I rose from the ground on legs that were no longer clumsy or unsure. They pulsed with strength and unimaginable capacity. I peered up at the ledge of the rooftop and bounced on the balls of my feet. That was all it took. I rocketed through the air. The wind whistled past my ears. The library rushed by in a blur. Three stories, no waiting. I landed gracefully on the edge of the roof.

I tarnished my spectacular entrance by letting slip a flabbergasted, "Whoa! Did you see that?! That was awesome!"

I glanced around for someone to second my emotion. The grisly scene before me shocked me back to the matters at hand.

Kendall was on her knees, her back pressed up against the clock tower, her hands tied behind her. In that position she couldn't deploy her wings and shield herself, a fact I was certain the Seeker had exploited. Her attacker was in human form. His spiky black hair the same shade as the pelt of the panther. His skin the grey pallor of death. He glared at me with frightening, solid black eyes. His hand was weaved into Kendall's long blond hair, yanking her head to the side to expose her bloodied neck. Cutting into her flesh was a glossy, ebony claw that curled out from his index finger. Blood dotted the front of her violet dress, but she was alive.

"Good." he sneered. "The other sister has arrived. Now we can figure out which is the Conduit and which gets to die."

Logic told me I was no match for him. My body seemed to know otherwise. It eagerly anticipated the fight. Seeing Kendall's terrified expression, I flicked a hint of the power I felt coursing through me at her. Her eyes widened, and a slow smile spread across her face. She peered up at her attacker.

"You know," she whispered. "I think you may be in trouble."

An enraged snarl ripped out of the Seeker. He released his hold on my sister and stalked toward me. "I don't care who or what you are. You are a puny, insignificant being, and I would like to taste your blood. " He spat the words at me as he morphed into the panther.

"Here kitty, kitty," I taunted and beckoned him with the curl of my finger.

The panther charged across the roof, his teeth bared. I inwardly trembled but stood my ground. About five yards away, he pounced. He flew through the air at me claws first. To my own astonishment, I acted on instinct and sprang into the air. My mind reeled as I corkscrewed around to deliver a round-house kick straight out of Fight Club. My foot connected with his jaw in a bone-crushing collision.

The wicked panther let out a yelp of pain as he skittered

backward across the roof. I landed softly, and rushed at him. With wide, anxious eyes, he watched me come. His gigantic claws struggled to get traction on the cement roof as he retreated. To gain ground, he morphed into human form. His jaw hung at a cockeyed angle; my kick apparently unhinged one side. Gross.

I put on the brakes as he approached the edge of the roof. He had nowhere to go. "You and I both know it's over," I stated. "Why don't you step away from the edge and we'll have a nice little chat about your demon buddies?"

His face sagged in a sickening grin. "I know who you are. Believe me when I say there is nothing but pain coming for you." With that, he did a reverse swan dive off the side of the building. I ran to the edge and watched in disbelief as he did a free fall toward the pavement. His arms and legs flailed until the moment when he exploded into a cloud of black smoke. It dissipated rapidly and left no trace of the black-eyed man.

I rushed to untie Kendall. She stared up at me in amazement.

"You okay?" I asked.

"I'll be fine, just surface wounds. I can heal myself as soon as I get my wings out. But, Cee, that was amazing! He killed himself just to get away from you. You're, like, a badass! How the heck did you do that?!"

"I have no idea! But it was cool!" I gushed. "Did you see the kicky, twirly thing I did? I don't know what that was, but it was friggin' sweet!"

"Yeah it was! There was only one problem."

"What?"

"Here kitty, kitty?" She raised one mocking eyebrow. "Really?"

"That was lame, I know. I'll work on my snappy one-liners for next time."

Her hands now free, Kendall rubbed her red, chaffed wrists. "That seems to be all you need to work on! It was a good thing the Gryphon picked today to soup you up. I was convinced I was a goner."

"I know," I grumbled. "I didn't think I was going to get here in time."

"But you did!" A wiggle of her shoulders and her wings appeared.

"Which was great because he didn't seem to care if he accidentally killed the chosen one or not. He just wanted the info. Barnabus must be coming down hard on these guys. The gloves are off."

"That means they'll send a replacement quickly." I looked her over and evaluated her injuries. Her neck wound was only skin deep. But her shoulder was sliced to the bone. "We've got to get your arm looked at Keni. It's bad."

"Not necessary," She grinned. "Watch this."

Her wings drew in around her, forming a tight, down cocoon. The feathers began to glow with a soft luminescence. After a moment, it subsided and Keni retracted her wings. Her injuries were gone. Not even a scar remained.

"Impressive."

"Not too shabby, huh? My dress on the other hand is DOA."

"Our calling has been detrimental to your wardrobe."

"Right?"

The sound of heavy footfalls landing on the rooftop behind us cut off our conversation. *I didn't kill the Seeker! He's back!* I whirled around and delivered an effective right hook without pausing to look.

My fist connected with its target as Kendall cried out, "Celeste! Stop!"

It was too late. I cold-cocked my brother right in the eye.

"Oh, crap! Sorry, Gabe!" I was going to have to leave a message. Gabe temporarily checked out.

He let out a shocked "*ooof*" then did a clumsy side-step. His eye instantly swelled shut. He would've hit the ground, but his sprawled legs locked up to prevent it. He hung his head and waited for the fog to clear. After a moment, he began slowly shaking his head. Blinking hard with his good eye, he peeked up at Kendall and me.

"Guess what, Gabe?" Kendall chirped weakly. "Celeste got her powers. Yay! How's your head?"

He let out a feeble grumble. I knocked a gigantic lion for a loop. If that doesn't stroke the ego, I don't know what does. I tried to look concerned while I internally gloated. "We should get you home and ice that eye. It's turning a lovely shade of purple. Do you think you can make it down from here?"

Gabe took a tentative step forward. His leg buckled under his weight. We rushed forward to help him back up.

"There's no way he can make it down," Kendall fretted.

"Can you fly him down?"

She shook her head. "No way. I'm like a quarter of his size. I couldn't lift him by myself. Unless ..." She looked my way with a speculative eye.

"Unless what?" I didn't like where this was going.

"You get an arm, I get an arm, and we jump."

I had been super strong for all of ten minutes. I had been afraid of heights a whole lot longer. "Isn't there a way into the building from up here? We could just break in and take the stairs. Easy squeezy."

Kendall rolled her eyes at me. "You would rather commit a crime by breaking and entering instead of just jumping down? You jumped up here you big wimp, you can jump back down. No big deal. And, if you do get hurt, I can heal you."

"Thank you, that's very reassuring," I muttered wryly. I turned to my stunned and befuddled brother. "Can you change back, Gabe? Make this a little easier on us?"

The lion half-heartedly raised his head, then let it drop again. I guess that answered my question.

"No biggie," An annoyingly up-beat Kendall shrugged. "We can just lift him up on his back legs. We'll drape his front paws around our necks."

141

That seemed like a monumentally bad idea. "Look at the size of him, Keni. No way can we keep hold of him while we jump."

"Sure we can, now that you have the super strength."

"Already you're taking advantage of my powers? If I'm doing all the heavy lifting, what the heck are you going to do?"

She put her hands on her hips. "I will make sure we have a smooth landing instead of crashing to the ground, if that's all right with you."

"Fine," I scoffed. "Let's just get this over with."

We finagled Gabe up onto his hind legs, draped his gigantic paws around our necks, and shuffled to the edge of the roof. I peered down over the ledge and got a nasty case of vertigo.

"Nope. Can't do it," I declared.

"Yes, you can," Kendall said. "Just don't look down. On the count of three, we're going to jump. Ready?"

"No, I changed my mind."

"One ..."

"Please don't make me do this."

"Two ..."

"I'm going to die."

"No, you're not. *Three!*"

I took the mother of all deep breaths, squeezed my eyes shut, and jumped. My hair whipped off my neck and lashed at my face as we plummeted toward the ground. To my shock and amazement, we landed without incident in the alley behind the library. My body reacted to the jump like I had done nothing more than hop off a curb.

No sooner had our feet touched the ground than a menacing hiss jerked our heads to the right. A pair of wild, luminescent green eyes peered at us from the shadows as it growled out its warning. My heart leapt into my throat with enough force that I almost choked on it. Another Seeker! I fumbled to free myself from Gabe's heavy arm when what turned out to be a stray cat charged past us. It sent a garbage can clattering to the ground in its panicked rush to get away from the lion that just fell from the sky.

Kendall's pink glossed lips split into a wide grin, "See? No biggie."

Easy for her to say...she wasn't the one having heart palpitations. Between the terrifying free fall and the "mysterious wild creature," I had a sudden need to go hide under my bed in the fetal position. "Let's get home," I gasped as I expelled the breath I'd been holding. "Immediately."

CHAPTER 23

Gabe had a score to settle. Actually, I think it was bigger than that. It was more like a deep-seeded vendetta against me for what he considered to be a "sucker punch."

For the last twelve hours, I had been forced to listen to him whine and moan about it. According to him, if he had been expecting it, I wouldn't have been able to touch him. Granted, I had limited fighting experience, but I was pretty sure people didn't normally give written warning before they threw a punch. Not to mention the guy's supposed to have cat-like reflexes, but whatever.

When Grams got home he even bellyached to her about it. She told him to suck it up and quit being a crybaby. Scoping out his black eye, she added, "Geez, Gabe you must bruise like a peach to get a shiner like that from a little, bitty thing like Celeste."

He glared daggers at me until Grams left the room. Then he snarled, "Tomorrow, when we go into the mountains to train, I'm kickin' your butt."

"I said I was sorry," I reminded him for the millionth time.

He scowled and shook his head. "Doesn't matter. Has to

happen."

I opened my mouth to protest when Kendall cut me off. "He's, like, on testosterone overload, Cee. Save your breath. You're gonna have to spar with him to shut him up."

The next day he could barely contain himself. His trash talk entered a whole new plateau. He probably would've resorted to insulting my mama if she wasn't his mama, too. I tuned him out. A maneuver I had perfected over the last eighteen years. We entered the clearing together where Alaina awaited us.

She gave us a maternal smile as we approached. "Good morning. I see Kendall is taking the first shift watching over your grandmother today. Gabe, we can start with some endurance exercise if that suits you?"

Gabe's eyes flicked to my face. Apparently Alaina didn't get a memo from the Gryphon about what took place last night. "Actually, Kendall isn't watching over Grams. She's running an errand, she'll be here soon."

Alaina's eyebrows drew in and her lips pursed in disapproval. "No one is watching over your grandmother? At any moment the Seeker could venture into her home searching for you. She could be hurt. This is not acceptable. One of you needs to get back there immediately."

Gabe threw his hands up, palms out. "Whoa. Chill out. Celeste finished off the Seeker last night."

A bird-like twitch of her head and Alaina's avian eyes focused on me. She examined me so intently that it made me fidget. Her gaze settled on my face. Whatever she saw there softened her expression and brought the grin back to her lips. "Our warrior has been awakened."

"Looks like," I blushed.

"That being the case," she steepled her fingers under her chin, "you can actually participate today. I suppose it would be a better use of our time to have you spar in preparation for the next Seeker who comes."

"*Yes!*" Gabe exclaimed and pumped his fist in the air.

"Hey, Gabe, can you give Alaina and me a minute please?" I asked. "Go warm up or something?"

He bounced up and down, shaking out his limbs. "I don't need to warm up. I was born ready for this!"

"That's great. Can we please have a sec?"

"Take all the time you need. It's not going to help!" He did his best tough guy saunter toward the creek.

"What is his posturing all about?"

"I accidentally punched him in the face last night and he's having a hard time coping with it."

"Ah, I see. What is it that is on your mind, Celeste?"

"I'm fairly certain he's going to fight dirty. His masculinity being called into question and all." I drew a line in the dirt with the toe of my tennis shoe. I was a "warrior" now. I wasn't supposed to be nervous about stuff like this anymore. "But—uh—yesterday was the first time I've ever been in a fight..."

"Come on, Cee! Wrap up the pep talk! It's not going to help anyway!" Gabe threw a left jab and right hook in the air.

"Just a minute!" I snapped.

"You are worried he is going to overpower you?"

"Completely. I have no idea what I'm doing."

"Trust yourself and the Gryphon. He has instilled in you the abilities. All you need to do is channel them. It will come as naturally as breathing or walking."

"Easy for you to say...you don't trip over your own feet on a daily basis," I muttered.

"You two can plan your mani-pedis later. Let's do this!" Gabe yelled.

"You know in my day, the men provided for and protected their families." Alaina reflected. "Their ability to do so successfully defined what kind of man they were."

"Are you telling me that for the sake of his fragile male ego, I should let him win?"

"Oh, goodness no!" She clarified and waved her hand at the thought. "He is being a pompous pig. By all means go knock his lights out."

I let out a heartfelt laugh. "Will do!"

"I will perch up there." Alaina pointed to the top of a tall maple tree overlooking the trail. "If I see anyone coming, I shall alert you. Please try to remember to listen for me."

"Don't worry, Alaina," Gabe smirked. "It won't take my full attention to knock her on her butt."

I snorted at his comment. "From what I saw yesterday, Gabe, you fold like a sheet of paper."

"You sucker punched me!"

"Not my fault you're slow."

He laughed and shook his head. "Oh, it is so on."

"I will be in the tree." Alaina morphed and flitted up into the branches to get out of striking distance.

Gabe and I squared off at opposite sides of the clearing. I hit a crouch first.

"I won't hold back if you don't," I offered, hoping that wasn't just me blowing smoke.

"Fine by me ... I've got no problem kicking your butt." He growled and fell down on all fours.

I wanted to get one last jab in before he transformed. "Maybe I could find a big ball of string to distract you. Whattya say, fuzzball?"

His voice dropped octaves as the change neared. "I say, I'm going to enjoy this."

The transformation seemed easier on Gabe now. It wasn't easier to watch. I couldn't help but crinkle my nose as his bones cracked and popped to allow his other form to emerge. Like a well-cared for Chia Pet, hair sprouted all over his body. It only took seconds before my brother disappeared and the tawny-colored lion stood before me. He let out an intimidating roar.

"Ooh, scary. Ya know if you lose again to a little girl like me,

147

maybe we should take that old game show host's advice and have you neutered."

Gabe didn't like that idea. He galloped straight for me, his fierce eyes fixated on my head. I matched his speed as I darted forward. As soon as he got within striking distance he sprung up to swipe at my face—which, by the way, I find rude. However, all his claws found was empty air. I spun down into a low swing kick and swept his back legs out from under him. He fell flat on his side, then leapt back to his feet.

"Less than a minute." I waggled my eyebrows at him. "I'm good."

He snarled his response.

"I tell ya what. I'll even give you the advantage." I shut my eyes and turned my back to the lion. "Go ahead. Take your best shot."

Yes, I was being arrogant. But I couldn't help it. I was thoroughly enjoying this.

I sensed it when Gabe ducked down. I knew his every move as his stomach skimmed the ground as he crept toward me. He was the perfect model of feline stealth, but I remained one step ahead of him. Silent as a grave, he extended his razor-sharp claws and swiped. At the last possible moment, I jumped into the air. I've never had a gymnastics class in my life, yet I managed a back-tuck with ease.

Gabe interrupted my evasion maneuver with a counter-assault. He sprang up and swatted at me. One of his dagger-like claws tore into my arm while I was in mid-rotation. He knocked me slightly off kilter, but I still managed a somewhat graceful landing. I assessed my sliced tricep. My slashed skin healed before the blood could spill. The flesh pulled itself together and left no blemish or mark.

Gabe's eyes bulged at my amazing disappearing booboo.

"I knocked you out. You sliced my arm. That makes us even."

Gabe's topaz cat eyes flashed. *"Nnooo wwaaayyyy ..."*

I lost my warrior posture and indignantly snapped straight up.

He'd been practicing talking in his feline form. It assaulted my ears worse than nails on a chalkboard. "Ah!" I wagged my finger at him. "None of that! That creepy voice sounds like Satan! Or a blender. Or a blender possessed by Satan. You start that up again and I'm leaving. Understand?"

He rolled his eyes and clamped his mouth firmly shut. With a pointed stare, he made it clear that he would adhere to my rule.

"Thank you. Now, where were we?" Simultaneously, we returned to our prowl. We trailed each other, both looking for an opportunity. Mine came when Gabe stepped wrong and gave me a straight shot at his ribs. I took advantage of it and bolted directly at him. He started to turn, but didn't make it in time. I hit him square in the midsection.

His air escaped in a loud "Huynh!"

I wrapped my arms around him and took him down, just as I had seen him do countless times on the football field. I bounced to my feet, bubbling with pride. My whole life I had been the wallflower, the awkward kid that watched from the sidelines just to spare herself the humiliation. For the first time, I came out on top. My happy dance was required. I bebopped around and gloated, until I noticed Gabe hadn't gotten up. He lay motionless on the ground where he fell. Fear coursed through me. I hurried over to find the burly lion gasping for air. I knocked the wind out of him, and he couldn't seem to reclaim it.

"Oh, geez! I'm so sorry, Gabe. You okay?" I bent down next to him, trying to figure out how to give CPR to a lion.

In an instant his breathing stabilized. His head lifted off the ground, and he grinned wickedly at me. A monstrous paw whacked me square in the chest and sent me tumbling. I turned my tumble into a back somersault and was back on my feet in seconds.

I shook my head in disdain. "I knew you'd fight dirty."

He pulled himself up to full height and roared. I gave him the evil eye then swooped in for another attack. I only made it two strides before the shrill call of an eagle stopped me in my tracks.

"Someone's coming!" I yelled to my brother.

I started one way, then darted the other, not quite sure what to do with myself. I settled for the log by the stream as my destination. I scurried over and sat down. I crossed my legs, sat up straight, and tried to look casual. I realized too late that my pose would seem odd for someone sitting alone in the woods. Gabe must have hidden by now. The rustle of leaves coming from the path told me I didn't have time to come up with anything else. Whoever the hiker was, he or she was going to find me sitting there looking like I was waiting for a bus. Brilliant.

Through the leaves, spiky, disheveled, platinum hair appeared. I didn't recognize who it was until she ducked under the branch in front of me and gasped.

"What the heck?! I'm going to have to claw my own eyes out! Gabe! Why?! What possible reason could you have for being *naked*!" Kendall exclaimed and covered her eyes.

Completely bewildered, I swiveled around. There stood Gabe, stark naked. The only thing he could cover himself with was his own hands. With a beet-red face, he cringed as if in pain.

I immediately spun back around and shielded my own eyes. "I could have happily gone my whole life without seeing that!" Sitting there with my hands over my eyes, I addressed our new arrival. "Kendall! You hacked your hair off!"

Her voice was muffled by her arms, "Actually, Marcie at the only beauty salon in town cut it for me. Do you like it?"

"Can't tell yet. Gabe, is it safe to look?"

"No!" he yelped. "I'm still standing here naked."

"Why? Why are you naked?"

"I don't know!" he snapped. "You said someone was coming, so I changed back. But I couldn't find my bag of clothes."

"Why didn't you just hide?"

Silence. Then, "I didn't think of that."

Kendall and I both erupted in laughter. "You ... thought of ...

naked, before ... hiding!" I choked out.

"Yes. Shut up. I'm going to change back now."

"Please do!" Kendall and I said in unison.

It only took a second before the Gabe-lion gave a rumble indicating that the need to avert our eyes had passed.

"Thank you! Now let's just hope my corneas can recover from that," I joked and dropped my hands. The giant cat snorted in response.

With the traumatizing image of my exposed brother gone, I checked out Kendall's new do. She looked totally different. She's one of those infuriating girls that could shave her head and still be gorgeous, so it wasn't a bad different. But, her long locks were gone. Now, purposely messy blonde spikes darted off her head in an array of directions.

"So? What do you think?" she asked expectantly. Before I could answer, she held up one finger for me to wait, then snapped open her wings. "There, now you get the full effect."

I evaluated the look for a minute. "You look like a punk rock angel."

Her eyes flashed. "Perfect!" She raised her hand in the air with her index and pinkie finger extended, then stuck her tongue out to complete her "rocker" look.

"What brought this on, Keni?" I chuckled.

A painful shadow crossed her face. "When I brushed my hair this morning, I knew I needed a change. Running the brush through my hair reminded me of the Seeker's hand being wrapped in it. He used it to hurt me. So, it had to go. At least for right now while the memory is still fresh."

The lion and I both nodded our understanding but said nothing. This was something she would have to work through to be able to put the whole ordeal behind her.

"So, how do we train with all three of us here?" I asked.

The incoming flap of glowing, transforming wings marked Alaina's arrival. "I can help with that. I would have come down sooner, but it did not seem appropriate." She looked at Gabe with raised eyebrows.

Come to find out, lions can blush. Or, at least this one could.

"That was some show." Was it my imagination or was her face flushed?

"One that I'm sure we can all agree we don't ever, ever want to see again." I ruffled Gabe-lion's mane. He ducked away then batted at me with the soft pads of his oversized paw.

"Here, here," Kendall agreed.

Alaina cleared her throat and pointedly changed the subject. "I have a special training exercise for all three of you." She expanded her wings wide, then reached behind her back and pulled out a small box.

"Where do you suppose she pulled that out of?" Kendall whispered to me. I stifled a giggle.

Alaina took the box to the dead center of the clearing and laid it on the ground. "The Gryphon gave me this for when you all had been activated."

Gabe, Kendall, and I gathered around. The deep burgundy box was exquisite, its faded paint complimented beautifully by shiny brass hinges and an intricate clasp on the front.

"Activated? What are we ... a phone card?" I asked.

She turned and flipped the fancy latch. "I meant that you each had active powers."

"Oh, he got us a present!" Kendall gave a little golf-clap.

Alaina sucked air in through clenched teeth. "Um, not exactly. Unless you consider three shadow monsters programmed to try to destroy you a gift."

"Wow, that's like the worst gift ever. Gift cards are always safe. He should've gotten us one of those." Kendall's funky 'do seemed to have added an edge to her humor.

Alaina smirked and continued on. "These phantom demons have been given the directive to attempt to overcome the three of you. Your challenge is to work as a team to get them back in the box."

"Are they going to try to kill us?" I asked.

Alaina folded her hands in front of her. "We need you to save the world, Celeste. That tends to work best if you are alive. They will fight relentlessly and possibly wound. They will not actually take your life. The whole point is to get you experience at working together. Understand?"

We nodded.

"Good. Let us begin." She flipped open the lid then quickly backed away from the box.

Grey fog erupted from the box like a geyser. "Any tips on how to defeat these guys?" The flap of her wings as she retreated to the safety of her branch was the only answer I got. "I'll take that as a no."

The thick haze continued to course out of the seemingly bottomless container. It compounded together to form a thick, solid wall of the grey smog. When the last of it finally spit from the box, we waited and watched for whatever nasty being was going to burst out at us. Nothing happened.

"Are … are we supposed to fight the big wall of fog?" A bewildered Kendall whispered.

Before I could answer, the haze started moving, swirling, and gathering into three distinct locations. "No, look, something's happening."

The fog came together to create three identical shapes—gargantuan, hulking, menacing bodies, their sizes double that of Gabe's human form. The freakishly large arms that took shape were the size of my entire body. A lump grew out of each set of bulky shoulders, forming a makeshift head. Empty holes with glowing, red centers were the closest they came to having eyes. A black slash echoed a crude mouth on each. Their formation complete, they moved with soldier precision into a line opposite us, standing side by side, slightly hunched, posed for battle.

"Well, that's alarmingly intimidating," I blurted out.

"Can we ask them to try for another shape? Like maybe fog bunnies?" Kendall peeped.

A low, rumbling growl came from the monsters. Then, in trained unison, they marched toward us.

"Here we go," I said.

Kendall whimpered and Gabe growled. Together, the three of us braced ourselves.

Gabe and I charged at them, leaving a hesitant Kendall behind. Gabe-lion sprang into a pounce at the same time I leapt into the air for a side kick.

It amazed me that my body knew how to do this. Before my little "upgrade," I tripped over my feet at the mention of physical activity. Now I jumped high enough into the air to be head level with the monsters with no difficulty at all. But my abilities didn't make me impervious to harm, as I found out when I passed right through the foggy creature and landed flat on my back with a painful thump. My own groans didn't drown out Gabe's howl of pain as he crunched to the ground not six feet from me.

I rolled to my side and saw the monster stomp straight at me. Still smarting from my fall, I didn't rush to dash out of the way. His balled fist would just slip right through me, so I saw no reason to move. I had time to regroup before I got up and played along with the little charade.

I noticed a second too late that his incoming fist suddenly had pallor and texture to it. The monsters could solidify. He punched me in the face with a fist bigger than my entire head. Black spots danced before my eyes and warmth dribbled from my split lip and bloodied nose. I curled into a ball and covered my face with my arms just in time for the next blow to come. The crunch and shooting pain that followed told me he cracked at least one of my ribs. I tried to shield myself as much as possible from the kicks and punches that came like rapid fire. Every exposed part of my body was sore from the beating I took.

I peeked through the cover of my arms to see Kendall. She

knelt on the ground, her wings encapsulating her. One of the monsters pounded away at her as well. I envied her impenetrable wings because they made the beating painless for her. As long as she kept her shield up, she would fare a lot better than Gabe and me. I couldn't see Gabe, but the occasional snarl and yelp told me he wasn't doing so hot either.

Stealing a look between her feathers, Kendall met my eyes. "You okay?"

"Ooof! Getting my butt ... *hunh* ... handed to me," I wheezed. "How's ... *ooww* ... Gabe?"

"Somehow he's still standing. He's battered but standing." A loud howl of pain echoed through the clearing. "Uh ... not anymore."

A scream tore from my chest as the creature delivered a sharp kick that must have cracked a rib. Searing pain stabbed into my side. That was one kick too many. Fury built in me, motivating me to get off the ground and put an end to all of this—just as soon as I figured out a way to move.

"Keni?" I called, my teeth grinding in pain. "Can you ... get to ... Gabe?"

She hesitated before answering. I assumed it was to assess the situation. I didn't risk another look toward her. Instead, I tried to find a way out from under the barrage of attacks from this nasty smog being. "I'll try," she answered, but her voice lacked conviction.

Her wings beat against the air, followed by a shrill, nonhuman wail. The howl caught the attention of my attacker, who paused and turned to look toward his troubled buddy. I rolled out of striking distance and put some much needed space between the bowling-ball-fisted monster and me. Rising onto my shaky legs, I had a moment of panic that they wouldn't support me. They did, but I was going to need some ice packs later. Lots of 'em.

I retreated to the edge of the clearing where I figured out what caused the creature's pained cries. The wind stirred up by

Kendall's wings dissipated his foggy form. He stumbled frantically to get away from her. Backpedaling, he tripped over something—the slack body of a lion. He lost his footing and fell, right over the box he emerged from earlier. His form evaporated into a heavy cloud which was sucked back in from where it emerged. I attempted a cocky sneer at this display of their weakness; however, as soon as I moved my battered face, it quickly turned into a wince of pain.

Seeing their friend disappear back into the box angered the remaining monsters. They bellowed deep, gravelly roars, then turned to Kendall and me for retribution.

"We need gale force winds, Keni! Now!"

She gave a sharp nod of understanding and lifted higher into the air. "I'm on it!" She circled the perimeter of the clearing, flying as fast as her inner eagle would allow. In a moment's time, she worked up a robust, continual wind.

The remaining monsters staggered, desperately seeking some sort of cover. They lost their footing repeatedly as their foggy legs blew out from under them. In an act of frustration one of the smog ogres gave up and solidified his entire form. He stomped after Kendall.

He didn't notice the head of the mighty lion rise up of the ground, and I'm sure he didn't see Gabe wink at me. Gabe sprang to his feet and charged the enormous, corporeal monster. A piercing howl escaped its slash of a mouth when our lion clamped down on its thick, grey leg. It thrashed around wildly, striking out at our Gabe-lion. His face took a beating, but his vise grip jaws never faltered. He dragged the flailing creature to the box. It disappeared inside, just like the first.

After seeing how we disbanded his comrades, the third fog thing tried to make an escape. Keni intercepted his departure by flying in low and beating her wings directly at him. He pivoted on his heel, back toward Gabe and me. With Keni low to the ground, he could stay in mist form as soon as he got some distance from her. An evil grin reminiscent of a jack o'lantern spread across his face. He could fight again, at least for a moment. He charged for Gabe, seeking some retribution. Unless he went solid, we couldn't get him.

I bolted toward Gabe on the other side of the clearing. "Let him hit you, Gabe!"

The brawny lion scowled at me and shook his head. "*Nooo!*"

"Take one for the team and let him hit you, you overgrown tabby!"

Gabe planted his feet and grit his teeth. The monster stomped up to him and arced back that sledge hammer of a fist. I saw the texture change from dense cloudy air to solid, bumpy skin. I jumped, kicking both feet straight out in front of me. My fast-flying feet hit the beast square in the middle of his back knocking him forward. The open box happened to be lying right there. I'd like to say I planned it that way, but it was sheer luck. In a swirl of smoke, the last of the monsters vanished. Its contents restored, the box snapped shut and locked.

Kendall landed, and the three of us tentatively approached the burgundy container, cautious that it might not be over. The sound of applause behind us confirmed it was.

"Very well done for your first time," Alaina encouraged.

"It sure didn't feel good." Something popped and sent a shooting pain through my face. My hands flew up. "*Oooowwww!* What the heck was that?!"

Kendall recoiled at whatever freaky thing happened to me. "It was a good pop, Cee. Your nose was broken and pointing in the wrong direction. It just fixed itself. Yay!" Her "yay" lacked any enthusiasm.

"Yeah," I said flatly. "That hurt like a …"

"I am very proud of you all," Alaina said. "Even when you were not faring well, you kept looking for ways to turn things around. That was impressive."

"And we learned how to take a punch. So yee-haw to that," I

said, gingerly rubbing my aching sniffer. I glanced at Gabe and Kendall. Kendall looked great, barely a hair out of place. Gabe looked rough. His head hung wearily, chunks of fur missing like he had mange. The eye I had blackened was swollen shut again and bruises peppered him enough to be visible through his furry hide. I could only imagine that I looked pretty rough myself. Every inch of my body hurt. I hoped my speed healing would get cracking, or it was going to be a painful drive home. "Those guys were tough. It was like a thousand times harder to get them to go 'poof' than it was with the Seeker. And he was actually willing to kill us!"

"What?" Alaina's wild and panicked eyes caught me off guard.

"Well … these guys didn't really want to …" I stammered, confused by her reaction.

"Not that! What do you mean the Seeker went 'poof'?"

"When he died, he went 'poof,' you know? Black cloud of smoke. Then he was gone. He just 'poofed'," I babbled.

All the color drained from Alaina's already milky skin. She spoke with a vacant, hollow tone. "Seeker's liquefy and evaporate when they die. However, when they teleport, they do so in a cloud of black smoke."

I heard the pounding of my heart ringing in my ears. I knew the answer to the question before I asked but hoped somehow I was wrong. "And if he teleported, he went …"

She met my eyes with a steely gaze. "To tell Barnabus. He knows who you are and where to find you."

I squeezed my eyes shut. "Keni, please tell me you saw Grams leave the house heading for some crazy, old lady fun today."

Her trepidation caused her voice to waver. "She's at home. She said she wanted to catch up on her stories."

The urgency of the situation made me forget my sore muscles and bones. "Get to the truck now!" I ordered. "We have to get home."

The three of us spun and sprinted for the truck. I paused when I realized Alaina wasn't following.

"You're not coming?"

She shook her head sadly. "My role is to guide you. This fight belongs to you, Gabe, and Kendall. I cannot stand beside you."

"Are we ready for this?"

"You have to be."

CHAPTER 24

Everything looked normal as we sped down Dole. The town still stood, so one of my fears got squelched. But as we neared Grams' street, red and blue flashing lights made my pulse race.

"Oh-no," Kendall whispered. She unfastened her seatbelt and slid forward to peer over the front seat.

A boulder of cold, hard fear settled into my stomach. "It's not Grams. It's not Grams. It's not Grams," I chanted to myself.

I turned onto our street and our fears were instantly transformed into reality. Four police cars surrounded our grandmother's house. Room for only one of them in the driveway meant two others parked on her lawn and the last in the road. Their lights flashed away, and yellow crime scene tape surrounded the tiny property. Kendall let out a choked sob while Gabe punched the roof of my truck hard enough to dent it. I must have switched into autopilot because I managed to park the truck without wrecking it. I felt numb from head to toe.

The neighbors stood outside watching. I opened myself up to

their feelings hoping the mood of the crowd would tell me things weren't as bad as they looked. Instead, I felt collective sorrow. My lip trembled and my heart sank.

You cannot fall apart right now, Celeste. Do you understand? I scolded myself. *Get out of the truck and get answers. You owe it to Grams to be strong.*

The pitiful gasps from the neighbors when I climbed out of the truck didn't escape my notice. I held my head high, clenched my jaw, and marched toward the house. I closed myself off from the wave of sympathy from the crowd before it could crash down on me. I couldn't risk crumbling beneath it.

I ducked under the yellow tape perimeter and heard, "Excuse me, Miss? I'm going to have to ask you to stay behind the tape." I looked up into the young officer's stern face. He had been at Ella's house too. When he recognized me, his face blanched. "Oh, Miss Garrett. Go on in. Captain Cooper's inside."

"Thank you." I continued toward the house without waiting for his response.

As soon as I stepped inside, my breath caught. It looked like a tornado tore through the living room. Grams' glass coffee table had been shattered. The wrought iron base of it ripped in two, the sides strewn to opposite corners of the room. Grams' curio cabinet leaned precariously against the arm of her leather chair, all its contents broken and embedded in the cushions. The ceramic angels that lived on a shelf above the couch did not survive the fall. Their ceramic limbs and assorted body parts were scattered around the room. Framed pictures of our family lay on the floor, crushed beyond recognition. The wall that divided the foyer and the living room—where Grams measured us when we were little and marked our growth with a pencil slash—sported a deep hole in the plaster. I cringed at the dimensions of the hole. It matched a human body. I prayed that was a coincidence.

Uniformed strangers milled around. They dusted for prints, took photographs, and collected evidence in little baggies, jotted down notes and all that other CSI stuff. A grey-haired man in a tan sport coat stood in the middle of the room, barking orders.

"I want this entire place dusted for prints. Mess like this, he couldn't have been careful about what he touched." The crunch of glass under my shoe spun him toward me. His moustache matched his hair. A hefty paunch around his middle strained the buttons on his shirt. His thick eyebrows drew together when he saw me. "Why isn't anyone patrolling the perimeter? I got people just wandering in!"

"Captain Cooper, my name is Celeste Garrett. I live here with my grandmother, Gladys."

His expression softened. He pursed his thick lips and inhaled deeply. I followed his gaze as he glanced around for a place for us to sit and talk. The living room window had also been demolished. There wasn't an inch of the room that wasn't decorated with glass shards.

Captain Cooper noticed my pained expression. "Why don't we go sit out on the porch?" He placed his hand on my shoulder and steered me back out the door.

Robotically, I sat in my usual rocking chair and gazed around at the vastly different scenery. It looked like one of those cop shows Grams loved so much. Gabe played the role of the angry family member. He took out his frustrations on a rookie cop that held no answers to Gabe's bombardment of questions. Kendall sought solace in the arms of a former love. Keith comforted her, our tragedy reuniting them. Alec, the steadfast reporter, nosed around eager to get to the bottom of this. The gawkers watched out of equal parts concern and morbid curiosity. The rocking chair next to me squeaked under Captain Cooper's weight. This was no show. I couldn't change the channel or turn it off. Like it or not, I had to sit here and wait for the good captain to tell me if my grandmother was alive or dead.

"Celeste, someone broke into your grandmother's home today. We think it started off as a simple robbery. A rarity here in

Gainesboro, but sometimes people get desperate." He paused for a moment and took a deep breath. "It seems the intruder didn't know your grandmother was home. Realizing she was must've startled him, and he panicked."

"What do you mean he panicked?" I asked somberly.

He ran a hand across his mustache and then over his mouth. Beads of perspiration dotted his forehead. "She was attacked."

The way he was tiptoeing around the details grated on me. "How bad is it?"

His bleak expression caused a lump in my throat I had to choke back. "It's bad. He roughed her up pretty severely. I don't know to what degree just yet. But we put her in an ambulance and rushed her to Nashville General. The last update I got was that she was slipping in and out of consciousness. She's in the ICU."

Tears threatened to spill from my eyes. I fought them back. I couldn't cry. Not here. Not now. Instead, I rose from my seat and started down the stairs, headed for my truck.

"Wait, Celeste!" he called after me. "I have a couple of quick questions for you."

"I have to go," I barely got the words out. He nodded, the possibility I may never see Grams alive again loomed between us.

"Just tell me," he pushed on. "Did your grandmother have any enemies that you know of? Anyone that would want to hurt her?"

Besides the three hundred year old demon hell-bent on killing me and destroying the world? Nope, that's about it.

Of course I couldn't say that out loud. Instead, I told him what he already knew. "This is a small town, Captain. I'm sure you know my grandmother almost as well as I do. You already know that everyone loved ... loves her." My voice broke when I accidentally referred to Grams in the past tense. He gave no further protests as I walked away.

Back on the other side of the yellow line, Kendall rushed toward me with Keith at her heels. Her eyes asked a million questions. A flush-faced Gabe pushed through the crowd to tower over me while he waited with barely concealed anxiety. Alec's face belied both his reporter's curiosity and his genuine concern for Grams and me.

I laid out the only details that mattered right now. "Grams is at Nashville General and she's alive. They can't tell us any more than that about her condition."

"We can be to the hospital in about a half hour," Gabe declared. He and I started for the truck. Kendall paused to say a quick goodbye to her rekindled love.

"Celeste!" Alec hollered after me as he ran to catch up.

Slightly agitated that he was delaying my rush to my grandmother's side, I spun on him. Before I could spout off my annoyance, he scooped me up off the ground in a tight bear hug. It would've been a nice moment to squeeze him back and revel in the comfort and security he offered. But I didn't. Instead I bristled at the act that threatened to expose my vulnerability at a time when I needed to be strong.

"I'm so sorry this is happening to you and your family," he whispered in my ear as he returned my feet to the ground. "If there is anything I can do to help, please let me know."

"Thank you," I mumbled.

He gave me a tight smile that didn't make it to his eyes. "No problem. Listen, I have to go to Memphis for a little while. Apparently there is some big story there. But if you need me for anything at all, I can be back in a flash. All you have to do is call."

"I will," I lied. His involvement with me would only get him hurt. Grams' current situation proved that. If I cared about him and wanted to keep him safe, I needed to stay far, far away from him.

"Good. Now go!" he prompted. I turned and dashed to my truck.

Gabe and Kendall were already buckled in waiting for me. I threw the truck in gear and sped off. My heart ached with my hope that the Nashville doctors could work miracles, but I slammed the gas pedal down in case they couldn't.

CHAPTER 25

We arrived at the hospital in record time. A bored-looking woman at the information desk told us that the ICU was on the second floor. Too impatient to wait on the elevator, we raced up the stairs. We located the nurses' station and asked for Grams' room number. A stern-faced nurse informed us her visitation had been restricted and we would have to wait in the waiting room until her doctor could speak to us.

The waiting room was a drab, depressing place. Someone tried to liven it up by hanging a relaxing seascape painting on the wall. It wasn't fooling anyone. This could never be a happy, relaxing room. We took a seat in the burgundy, padded chairs and stared numbly at the television mounted on the wall. With the volume turned down low, we couldn't hear it at all. Not like that mattered.

"Should we call Mom?" Gabe asked.

"After the fact," I said.

"She's going to be pissed that we didn't call her right away."

"If we call her now, she's going to jump on the first flight out to get here. Barnabus could pay her a visit, too."

166

He leaned back in his chair and let his head fall back against the wall. "After the fact."

Keni picked at a loose string on her pink cotton shorts. "If I can get in there, I can heal her."

"We would have to figure out how to hide your wings and that glowy thing you do, plus explaining to the doctors how their patient was miraculously healed," I pointed out.

"I'm not going to sit here and let her die," Kendall hissed through her teeth.

I reached over and squeezed Keni's hand. "No, *we* won't. We'll wait and hear what the doctors have to say. If we have to get you in there to heal her then that's what we'll do. One way or another, we aren't losing her today."

If we haven't lost her already, my mind added.

We hadn't been sitting there long when a short, balding gentleman in bright blue scrubs strolled in.

"The Garrett family?" he said directly to us. We were the only people with the misfortune of being in the ICU waiting room at the moment. We rose in unison as he approached.

"I'm Dr. Allyn." He extended his hand to each of us. "I've been treating your grandmother. She is your grandmother, correct?" We all nodded in agreement.

"How is she?" Gabe shoved his fidgety hands into the pockets of his khaki shorts.

Dr. Allyn's face gave nothing away. No shadow of sadness, no glimmer of hope in his eyes, nothing but a strong expression of knowledge and understanding. "Your grandmother has been through quite an ordeal, but we were able to get her stabilized. To start with, she had numerous abrasions to her face and torso that had to be stitched up. Her right arm was broken in two locations. Both were clean breaks, so we set them, and they should heal nicely. With her age, she may require some physical therapy to retain full mobility of that limb. The biggest concern right now is from the blunt force trauma to her head. Very likely she has some swelling to her brain. We don't yet know the severity of it. We performed a spinal tap and a CAT scan to get some solid answers. She's conscious now, which is a good sign. But we won't know exactly where we stand until we get the tests back. Right now things could still turn on a dime."

"What are the best and worst case scenarios?" I inquired crossing my fingers behind my back that the word "death" didn't come out of his mouth.

"There are numerous outcomes, all having to do with the severity of her injury," Dr. Allyn explained. "If the swelling is minimal, she could just have a mild concussion and nothing more. Obviously, that's what we're hoping for. If the pressure on her brain is at a moderate level, she could have problems with her memory. She may have difficulty with her speech, walking, hand-eye coordination, things of that nature. With a high level of swelling, she's at risk of slipping into a comatose state. There are measures we can take to try to alleviate the pressure. But it would become imperative we get it under control."

"When will we know more?" Kendall's voice cracked.

The doctor laid a comforting hand on her shoulder. "I put a rush on the results, so it shouldn't be long. The minute I know something, I'll report back to you. You let me do the worrying about her, okay? After all, it is my job." His warm smile reminded me of my grandfather, which made it only seem right that he was looking after our Grams.

"Can we see her?" Kendall asked, her eyes red-rimmed and teary.

"I'll let one of you go in." The doctor's eyes shifted between us. "Just for a little while. Then she needs to rest."

"Who should go?" I asked.

"You," Gabe and Kendall answered in perfect unison.

"Why me?"

"Because Kendall won't be able to control certain impulses," Gabe said with the raise of his eyebrow to express his hidden meaning. "And I ... don't handle stuff like this well."

"Okay."

I followed the doctor down the brightly lit hall to a private room with the door shut.

"This is her room. Go on in. I'll give you two some privacy." He gave me the compassionate doctor face again, then turned and strode to the nurses' station. I took a deep breath before I pushed the door open.

I gasped at the battered and bruised version of my much-adored Grams lying on the hospital bed. Deep black and purple bruises covered every inch of exposed skin. Stitches held together a wound on her cheek and another on her forearm. The opposite arm was wrapped from wrist to shoulder in a heavy cast. Tubes and cords plugged into her all over. She looked aged, frail, and not at all like my spry, feisty grandmother. Barnabus would pay for this. He could count on that.

I hesitated at the door. She seemed to have gone back to sleep. I didn't want to wake her. I thought about going back to the waiting room and letting her rest. Before I had come to a decision, her sleepy eyes fluttered open.

"Celeste," she rasped in a drowsy, medicated voice.

I put on a big, reassuring smile and approached the side of her bed. "Hey there. How are you feeling?"

She groaned before answering. "Like I got hit by a truck. But did you see my doctor? What a dish, huh?"

I couldn't help but laugh. "Yeah, Grams, he's a hottie."

"Hands off," she murmured drowsily. "I'm calling dibs."

"No problem...he's all yours," I assured her. Venturing cautiously, I asked, "Grams, do you remember what happened?"

Her heavy lids fell shut again. Her eyebrows drew together. "It's just kind of a blur."

"Just remember what you can."

Her eyes remained closed as she began, "I was watching my stories. They were getting really good. Hailey found a cursed

169

necklace that allowed a demon to possess her. Then, I heard a loud thump against the window. At first I thought a bird flew into it. But when I looked up, the whole thing just shattered. I barely had time to cover myself. A man, wearing some sort of medieval costume, jumped through the broken window. He had one normal eye, but the other was solid black. He grabbed my arm and yanked me up out of my chair. He screamed something at me. What was it he said? Something about power. Where was my power, maybe? I told him to check the fuse box or get an extension cord. Then, something hit me. The whole side of my body hurt, bad enough that I think I blacked out for a minute." My stomach rolled. That explained the hole in the wall. He must've thrown her into it. "I woke up on the floor with my whole body hurtin'. The most intense pain came from my arm. It was twisted behind my back. His voice changed. It was like a hiss when he asked me … something. Something urgent. Oh, why can't I remember? It scared me to death. How could I have forgotten?"

She scowled as she fought to remember. Then her eyes snapped open wide. She stared at me in horror. "Oh, no! Oh! I remember! Honey, it was you! He knew your name! He was looking for you, Celeste!"

I knew full well that Barnabus was after me. However, hearing the words and seeing the impact it had on my Grams gave me goose bumps all over. I shook it off and concentrated on comforting my grandmother. "It's okay, Grams. I'm safe. See? Fit as a fiddle. Nothing to worry about."

"You didn't see this person, Celeste. I know this sounds crazy, but I don't think he was human. He was too strong. And his face, it seemed to … change."

I wanted to reach out to her, to soothe her frazzled state with a hand on her shoulder or a kiss to her forehead. But the battle scars that peppered her skin made me hesitant to touch her. I didn't want to hurt her more. I settled for patting her hand. "I'm going to be okay, Grams. I promise. I can take care of myself. I'm a tough chick, just like you."

"No, you don't understand, Celeste," she said sternly. She attempted to sit up, winced in pain, and then settled back onto her pillow. "This is different. You need to run. Do you hear me? Run. This guy is crazy as a bed bug and he *will* hurt you. There is money tucked in my sock drawer at home. Go get it. Take every last dollar. Grab your Gabe and Kendall and run!"

I glanced around the room. An extra IV pole sat in the corner. I retrieved it and brought it over by my grandmother.

"Just watch," I said softly.

Grams lips formed a thin, straight line. She looked confused, annoyed, and frustrated, but nodded and waited. I grabbed each end of the metal pole and bent it into a perfect circle. The metal screamed as it gave way to my grip. It molded in my hands like silly putty. I held it up for her to see.

"Shoddy craftsmanship," she stated, but doubt fluttered across her face.

I shook my head. "Solid metal."

Confusion drew her smudged, penciled-in eyebrows together as she looked back and forth from the misshapen pole to me and back again. When her gaze settled on me, she peered at me as if we'd never met.

Shifting uncomfortably, I muttered, "See, I told you I was strong."

She gawked at me, a tiny smile playing across her lips. "I'll say. You definitely didn't get that from my side of the family."

I leaned the pole against the wall then returned to my place at her side. "Like I said, you don't have to worry about me."

"I don't know what it is that you just did there. I'm sure you and I are going to need to have a conversation about that at some point. But right now, you need to burn rubber. Because strong won't be enough, Celeste. You need to scram, just steer clear of Memphis. I told him you had left Gainesboro and headed off to college. He took your Rhodes pamphlet when he left. He was going there to find you. Now is your chance to disappear. Go to Florida, Alaska, Timbuktu, I don't care. Just promise me that the three of you will stick together and get far away from here."

"I promise, Grams. We'll get far away from here." About four hours away from here, to Rhodes College.

My grandma nodded. Her whole body went slack against the pillow. She had drained her limited energy reserve trying to get through to me. "Where will you go?" she asked sleepily.

Before I had to lie again, Dr. Allyn gave a soft knock on the door and then entered the room. "Good news," he smiled. "Test results came back indicating that the swelling is minimal. You probably have a heck of a headache, but that's the worst of it. You're going to be fine. You're a strong woman, Ms. Garrett."

"I'm fit too. If you don't believe me, just check out the back door of this hospital gown," my grandmother flirted through her haze.

"Grams!" If it was possible to die of embarrassment, I would've keeled over right then. Dr. Allyn blushed and grinned like a school girl. Suddenly, I was very uncomfortable in that room. *Don't I have somewhere to be, or a demon to kill?*

"Maybe another time." The good doctor grinned back. *Unbelievably, unequivocally icky.* "Right now it's time for another dose of your pain meds and some much needed rest."

"That would be great. My arm's achin'," Grams admitted.

I gave her a feather-light kiss on her forehead. "Rest up."

"Call me and let me know where you end up. I love you," she whispered.

"I will. Love you too, Grams." I gave her one last wave before I left the room.

Right before it shut behind me I heard Dr. Allyn exclaim, "What the blazes happened to the IV pole?"

"Been like that since I woke up," Grams answered.

Did I mention my Grams rocks?

CHAPTER 26

Gabe and Kendall met me in the hallway.

"How is she?" they both asked.

"She's in pain but still has the strength to hit on her doctor, so I'd say she's gonna be fine. But ..." I shot a quick look around. This was too populated a locale for this conversation. I jerked my head toward the unisex bathroom. We filed in together and locked the door behind us.

"We could've waited to get the update until after you did your business," Gabe teased and jerked his head in the direction of the toilet.

"No time for Gabe-isms right now," I scowled. "Barnabus specifically asked her where I was. She did us a favor and told him I had already left for college, which means we now know exactly where he is—Memphis."

As soon as the word left my mouth a blaring siren went off in my brain. Alec's parting words to me: "I have to go to Memphis for a little while. Apparently there's some big story there."

I tried to be optimistic. It's a big city. The odds were slim that he would be anywhere near Rhodes. He should be fine. Most likely. Probably. Hopefully. Crap.

"Celeste? Where'd you go?" Kendall waved her hand in front of my face.

"Sorry." Best to worry about one thing at a time. "Barnabus isn't restricted by rules and orders like the Seekers are. He has no problem hurting or killing people. We learned that the hard way. So we need to stop him. He wants a war? I say we take it to him. Tonight."

They fell silent as my words sunk in.

Gabe pushed himself off the sink he had been leaning against. "Hells yeah. I'm in."

"He brought the fight to our doorstep. Now we end this," Kendall agreed. "So, guide us—oh, Chosen One. What do we do?"

I flipped my phone open to check the time. Eleven o'clock. The drive to Memphis would get us there around two a.m. First, we needed to know what we were walking into. "Keni, you could make the flight to Memphis in half the driving time. But can you do it without being seen and scaring people?"

"It's overcast and pitch black outside. As long as I stay above the clouds, it would, like, totally eliminate the risk of people seeing me and thinking it's judgment day."

"Awesome. Get to Rhodes and scope out exactly where Barnabus is hiding. Find out as much as you can. What this dude looks like, how many men he brought with him, what weapons they have, if they display any powers, anything that might help. But stay out of sight! Don't do anything stupid, like get yourself caught." My role as the leader felt surprisingly comfortable. "Gabe and I will drive there and meet up with you. Once we get the stats on what we are facing, we can come up with a battle plan."

Gabe's lip curled up in a growl. "I could run there, Cee! Let the lion stretch his legs."

I put one hand on my hip and looked up at him in exasperation. "You can't run seventy miles per hour. We take the truck."

174

"You're bossy now that you're the Conduit," he grumbled.

"Is that a problem?"

"Nope, just saying."

"Good. Then saddle up, gang. It's time for a showdown."

They looked at each other, then erupted in giggles and snorts of laughter.

"Exactly which Earp brother are you supposed to be?" Gabe taunted.

"Shut up. Let's just go."

CHAPTER 27

If this were a movie, we'd be mid-battle right now, I thought to myself as I watched the numbers tick by on the gas pump. Movies never showed the superhero stopping for gas. It went inspirational speech—or in my case a paltry excuse for one—then the epic battle. Never did they show the Batmobile at the Gas-N-Go. Alfred probably handled all that kind of stuff for the Caped Crusader. I needed an Alfred. If this turned into a permanent gig, I should look into that.

The gas station door chimed and Gabe came out. His arms overflowed with chips, beef jerky, and a two liter of pop.

I gaped at him in slack-jawed astonishment. "What are you doing?"

"What?" he asked. "It's a long drive, so I got snacks."

"We're not going on a road trip to an amusement park! We're facing the forces of darkness, remember?"

"Yeah, so? I'm hungry," he shrugged. "It's like before my games, there's no point in getting my game face on until I get there. In the meantime—road trip!"

"I bet Robin never made Batman stop for chips," I muttered

under my breath as I returned the nozzle to its resting place on the pump. I turned back toward the truck and saw a spiky blonde head bop around the side of the building. "Kendall! You're supposed to be halfway to Memphis by now!"

She threw her hands up. "I'm going; I'm going! I just had to stop to pee. It's a long flight."

I squeezed the bridge of my nose between my fingers and shook my head. We had to be the lousiest warriors ever.

Gabe rolled down my driver's side window and leaned out. "What are you waiting on? We goin' or what?"

Batman had it easy. He was an only child.

CHAPTER 28

Gabe fell asleep while I drove. We were on our way to face an army of demonic forces the likes of which we—or quite possibly anyone—had never seen. Yet there he was, slumped in his seat, snoring like a chainsaw. He probably ate himself into a junk food induced coma. He still clutched the two liter in his hand and chip crumbs decorated the front of his shirt. Sure it was a long, monotonous drive. But it seemed the simple fact that we might *die* would keep him awake. Dozing behind the wheel wasn't a problem for me at all. The closer we got to Memphis, the tighter I gripped the steering wheel.

We pulled into the college parking lot in the wee hours of the morning. Sunrise was only a few hours away. Night still held a stronghold. The darkness combined with the fact that a malicious man waited here to kill me made the nice, scenic campus an ominous and foreboding place. My mind conjured up scenes from every scary movie I had ever watched. Any minute now the dark, foreshadowing music would start up and the killer would jump out at me.

The added security of having Gabe awake suddenly became crucial. I smacked at his arm. "We're here. Wake up."

"Hmmm." He groaned and stretched. His voice heavy with sleep, he failed miserably at sounding awake and alert. "All right, let's get this party started. How do we find Kendall to get the scoop?"

"Uh ... I don't know. We don't want to risk calling any attention to her or us. We need to be subtle."

"Like what? Doing bird calls?" Gabe scoffed.

"That way would be a heck of a lot more discreet than calling her cell. She never turns her Glee ringtone to silent. I think it goes against her entire belief system."

"Hey, do you have a flashlight?"

"No. Why?"

"We could have shone it into the sky like the Bat Signal."

"Maybe next time. For now I say we go with bird calls."

My brother fought back a grin. "We're not the best at this are we?"

"Not even close."

"Think we'll get better with time?"

"For the sake of the world, I really hope so," I admitted.

"Okay," Gabe relented. "I can do an owl or a pigeon. Which is it?"

"It's night time. Go with owl."

"Owl it is."

Gabe reached for the door knob, but stopped short when a dark, shadowy figure landed on the hood of my truck. We both froze as the small truck shook from the impact. My breath caught, and my heart temporarily forgot how to beat.

Was the fight going to start so soon? Without any lead in or preparation? I was nowhere near ready! Shouldn't I have stretched or something first?   Plus, there was the added vulnerability of being trapped in an enclosed space. Barnabus could tear our heads off before we stepped out of the truck! That is if head rippage offage was one of his abilities—there was so much I still didn't know!

Next to me, Gabe snarled as his teeth lengthened. His skin began to churn. His bones snapped and set as he began his transformation.

"Don't change in my truck!" I screamed at him. "You'll tear the whole thing apart!" Wrong thing to be worried about right then, I know. Especially when the figure began to stoop toward my windshield. In a few short seconds we would be looking into the face of evil.

Or not.

Kendall mashed her face up against the glass and gave herself a pig nose. "Hey, guys!" She grinned. "What took you so long?"

Gabe growled at her, but stopped his transformation.

"I'll hold her down you bite her head," I suggested to Gabe, only half kidding. Climbing out of the truck, I poured my annoyance on thick. "You better have some useful info for us."

"That I do. And I have to say I, like, totally loved my little covert op. Made me feel very secret-agenty!"

"So what did you learn, Double-O Dense?" Gabe asked as his fangs retracted.

"There was a man with long red hair, uber old-fashioned clothes, and a cape heading into the theater."

"Someone wearing a cape heading into the theater? Are you sure he wasn't an actor in costume? He could have just been going to rehearsal," I suggested.

"Well, he could have been. If they're having rehearsals at two a.m. and are going to use the unconscious person he had flung over his shoulder as a prop."

"Now there's a hostage?" Gabe pulled his shirt off and threw it in the truck.

Kendall nodded solemnly.

"This just keeps getting better."

"Any sign of the army?" I asked.

"I haven't seen or heard them. I assume the long-haired, freaky guy was Barnabus. For all I know the army could have already been in the theater waiting for him. I can't say for sure that he's alone," Kendall admitted.

We really didn't have much to go on here. "Did he demonstrate any of his powers?"

Her blonde spikes didn't budge as she shook her head. "Nothing other than strength. The ... person he was carrying is a good-sized guy and he tossed him around like it was nothing."

I couldn't help but notice her hesitation. She purposely held something back. "What aren't you telling us, Kendall?"

She quickly flicked her gaze away from me, adjusted her shirt, and avoided make eye contact. "Nothing."

"Wow, you are just the worst liar ever," Gabe stated. "And you're a theater buff?"

"Spill it, Keni. Now."

Hesitantly, she brought her head up and sighed deeply. "Keep in mind, I'm not one hundred percent positive about this. The guy had his head down and was all limp and stuff so I couldn't tell for sure."

"Couldn't ... tell ... what?" I asked. I felt the muscles in my jaws tense.

"The hostage. Celeste, I think it's Alec."

I should've been surprised. I wasn't. Of course he would end up in the middle of this he made the fatal mistake of trying to get close to me. Barnabus was systematically attacking the people I cared about. I needed to end this or resign myself to wearing a sandwich board for the rest of my life that reads:

Get Close to Me
and Get Knocked Out by
a Cranky 300 Year Old Demon!

Determination dripped off of me as I declared, "We have to get him out. What's the best way in?"

"There's a door around back. If it is anything like the theaters back home, it will lead backstage. That'll give us the element of surprise," Kendall reported.

"Good. Let's go," I said.

We averted our eyes as Gabe ducked behind the truck to strip down the rest of the way and morph into the impressive, tawny lion. Kendall expanded her wings and took on her own majestic splendor. I glanced down at my t-shirt and cut-off sweatpants. Suddenly, I felt very underdressed. If the idea of myself in a superhero costume didn't give me the willies, I may've considered it. No skin-hugging spandex for me. I would make my peace with my grubby clothes.

Our odd trio—the lion, the angel and...me—came together. Cloaked by darkness, we made our way across the sleeping campus with determined strides and steeled nerves. For the most part.

CHAPTER 29

Bypassing the fancy, arched entrance of the theater, we crept through the trees and brush to the rear door. It was nothing more than a service entrance, which I automatically assumed would be locked.

"Do we kick it in?" I asked.

"Before we destroy property and stuff, maybe we could check to see if it's unlocked," Kendall replied. Gabe snorted and nodded.

I held my breath as I tried the door. It opened easily and without setting off any blaring alarms. I started to expel a sigh of relief when Gabe gave a low growl beside me. "What?"

"Unnn-llokked," he grumbled in his menacing vibrato.

I stared into the pitch black doorway that gave away no clues as to the building's contents. "Maybe we're not as unexpected as we hoped."

Gabe pushed past me and led the way into the darkness. If the gigantic lion with razor sharp teeth wanted to lead the way, I was totally okay with that. I followed close behind him. Keni brought up the rear. Gabe's slow, shuffle-footed steps told me even his feline night vision was being put to the test against the thick, heavy darkness. With no hint of light anywhere, I didn't realize he stopped moving until I smacked into him.

"Ooof!"

"Ssshhhhh!" Kendall shushed in my ear.

"Heeeerrrrrre," Gabe rumbled.

Something lay up ahead that only he could see. To get up to his line of sight, I placed one hand on his back and followed by touch up to his head. I grabbed Kendall's hand to drag her along with me. A sliver of light shined through a gap in the heavy stage curtain.

"The footlights are on," Keni whispered.

It was the middle of the night, the backdoor was unlocked, and the lights were on. Combine that with the fact that it was off-season for the campus, and there was only one answer. Barnabus had lured us right where he wanted us.

"It's a trap." My mind clicked away at what our next move should be. Barnabus staged every element. He certainly had to know we were there. Fighting under his terms would give him yet another advantage. Running suddenly didn't seem like such a bad idea as long as we could snatch Alec first.

Still worried about the possibility of facing an entire army, I crept toward the curtain. I cautiously peeked around the heavy fabric. My vantage point allowed me to see more than half of the theater and the entire stage. It was empty. The space out of my view wouldn't accommodate a horde of people. But Barnabus might be there.

I turned back to Gabe and Keni. "His army isn't here."

"So what do we do?" Kendall leaned in so I could hear her hushed tone.

"The odds are not in our favor." My skin prickled with anxiety. "I say we find Alec and then run like heck. If we can get Barnabus on our turf, we can give ourselves an edge."

"Back to the mountains?" Kendall asked.

I nodded even though she couldn't see it. "We've been

spending so much time there, we know the area. And we don't have to worry about innocent people getting hurt."

"Hooowww?" growled Gabe.

"We'll just have to watch each other's backs like we did with the fog monsters. Keep our eyes open and our feet moving. What do you think?"

"Let's do it." A rush of air indicated Keni had expanded her wings out wide behind her.

Gabe snarled his agreement.

My heart thudded in my chest as I spun toward the lights. I replaced my trepidation with determination as my foot touched the polished wood stage. Speed and tenacity was key if this was going to work. With Gabe and Kendall behind me, I approached the center of the stage, scanning every inch of the theater. I saw nothing but rows and rows of empty seats. Even my former blind spot sat vacant.

My spine tingled as my eyes fell on the orchestra pit directly in front of the stage. As outward appearances go, it was a perfect hiding spot. But that wasn't why my skin suddenly crawled. There was something down there. I knew it. Something lurked in the deep shadows of the brick cavity. I slunk in the direction of it, crouching low as I approached. Mere steps from the edge, I saw a flutter of movement. I froze. My hands balled into fists so tightly my nails dug into my palms.

A hand shot out of the darkness, clawing desperately at the brick wall. My heart skipped a beat and my bladder threatened to fail. Another hand hurriedly followed suit. The battered and scraped hands found an edge to latch onto and held tight. Disheveled, strawberry-blonde hair, streaked with blood, briefly appeared, then vanished as he lost his hold.

"Alec!" I fell to my knees to extend my hand down to him. "Give me your hand!" I glanced over my shoulder at my sister. "Kendall, help me pull him out!"

"What the heck do you need my help for?" She questioned as if

I had somehow forgotten my own abilities.

"One second, Alec! We're going to get you out!" I spun on my momentarily dense sister. Through my teeth, I hissed, "As far as he knows, I'm just a normal girl that cannot lift a grown man with one hand, remember? So, help me."

"Oh! Right!" she agreed and crossed the stage toward me.

The large paw of a jungle cat blocked her way. Gabe jerked his head in the direction of her wings. Catching his meaning, she swiftly drew them in. As she came to kneel beside me, Gabe-lion slunk back behind the thick curtain. That was for the best. The last thing we needed right then was his appearance to startle an unsuspecting Alec.

Kendall and I reached down for our friend. With the lights on the stage and none in the pit, it was impossible to see exactly where Alec was. "Alec, can you grab our hands?" I asked. I felt a weak grip close on my fingers. I grabbed it firmly with one hand, wrapping the other securely around his wrist. I looked at Kendall, "You got him?"

"Yep." With that, we both heaved him up out of the hole.

He landed on his knees on the stage, which gave me a clear view of the wound on the back of his head. His hair was matted together with blood, the hair and skin torn away in a spot the size of a half-dollar. I felt myself turn green as I assessed the large gash and the bloody mess surrounding it. It became crucial I distract myself by examining Alec's condition elsewhere. I found no other visible injuries.

"Are you okay?" I asked.

"I think so," he slurred, a clear sign to the contrary. He rolled, or more accurately fell, from his knees onto his rear. On his face was the same dazed and confused look Gabe had worn right after I socked him in the face. "We have to quit meeting like this," he garbled and tried to stand.

Keni and I grabbed his arms to steady him. "How's that?"

"In mid-head injury," he laughed weakly.

With Alec in our possession, we could move on to step two of our plan—run. Barnabus hadn't shown himself yet. Maybe, just maybe, he didn't see us come in. He could be on an evil guy coffee break or something. I didn't care what was keeping him. I just wanted to make a quick getaway.

"Let's go," I said to Kendall. We completely supported Alec's weight. His arms hung limp around our necks.

"Where are we going?" Alec murmured.

In retrospect, I should've just said we were leaving, but instead I made the error in judgment of telling him, "We're taking you to the hospital."

He had been shuffling along with us but instantly planted his feet and became immoveable dead weight. "No way. You didn't go to the hospital when you hit your head. I'm not going either."

"Your injury is way worse than mine was."

"Nope. Not goin'," he declared stubbornly.

"You might have a concussion or need stitches," Kendall argued as she readjusted his arm to get a better grip.

"I said the same thing to your sister." Alec tried to make his wavering voice sound firm.

"Okay," I tried negotiating. "I told you I would go to the hospital if my Grams said I needed to. So let's go see her and see what she thinks." We didn't have time for this. If Mister Bigshot Reporter didn't start cooperating, I was going to toss him over my shoulder and carry him out.

"Nice try," Alec said. "Your Grams is in the hospital."

"Celeste, we gotta go!" Kendall exclaimed urgently, her eyes frantically scanning the room.

"I know!" I shot back. "Alec, what does your Mom do?"

"She's a beautician. Her name's Marcie."

"Oh ... hey!" Kendall perked up, pointing to her new 'do. I glared in response. We didn't have time for her "hey, small world" moment.

"Great," I stated. "We'll go see your mom. If she thinks you need to go to the hospital, you go. Okay?" This made no sense. His mother was a good three hours away. I hoped his head injury had him foggy enough that he wouldn't remember that.

"Okay," he relented and unplanted his feet. With him cooperating, we scurried for the exit, practically dragging him. He noticed and slurred out, "What's the rush?"

We ignored him and kept moving. The door was in sight. Our chance for escape only a few steps away. Then the theater went black.

"Whoa, did I just pass out?" Alec asked.

"No. The lights went out." Every muscle in my body tensed. The darkness was no coincidence. It wasn't a friendly janitor flipping a switch. It was a man with murder on his mind, letting us know that the games were about to begin. "Kendall, get Alec outside. I'll go see about those lights."

"No way. You need me to help you turn the lights back on." She adapted her argument for Alec's sake.

"Get him out of here, then come help me find the switch."

"You two are making an awfully big deal out of the lights. Aren't we leaving anyway? Leave 'em off; conserve energy," Alec garbled.

"No can do, Alec. But we'll take care of everything, all right?" I reassured him.

"Whatever," he murmured.

"He definitely needs a doctor. Stay with him, Keni. Come on, Gabe." Fur brushed my leg as my lion bodyguard fell into step beside me. Together we strode back out onto the stage.

This time we didn't have the aid of the footlights as we ventured across the lofty stage. Each step we took in the thick darkness was made with the utmost caution, on high alert for when Barnabus would strike. Without warning, a blinding spotlight snapped on, pointed directly at me. I brought my arm up to shield my eyes and squinted to see past the offending light. Its brightness blinded me to anything beyond it.

From the shadows came a voice. "So you are the one. The little girl I have been searching for. My mentally-deficient minion was right. We did calculate your age wrong. No matter now though, is it? All that really matters is that I have you."

His voice sounded shockingly ordinary for a three hundred-year-old villain. Not that my legs weren't trembling in fear because, believe me, they were. I mustered up every ounce of courage I had to reply, "I knew you were a coward when you attacked my grandmother. But are you really so scared to face me that you have to hide?"

The theater boomed with the echo of his loud guffaw. With laughter still thick in his voice, he answered, "Oh, don't worry about that. I'll show myself soon enough. I'm thrilled you have a feisty spirit though. It'll make killing you much more enjoyable."

"You'll have to go through us first," Kendall stated as she strode up beside me. Gabe took a step forward as well, his lip curling up in a threatening snarl.

Under my breath, I whispered to Keni, "Did you get Alec to safety?"

"Yeah."

"You two?" Barnabus chuckled. "You two are merely pawns not even worthy of my time." In the blink of an eye, Gabe and Kendall both went flying through the air in opposite directions. No one and nothing touched them. Yet it seemed an unseen force hooked them around their midsections and flung them across the room. They each disappeared behind the sides of the stage curtain. Two heavy thumps followed by loud groans let me know that their unexpected rides ended painfully. I stood there alone, vulnerable and exposed. "But you, ah, you are the real power. The Conduit. The chosen one—bound to all that is good. Most importantly, you're my key to unlimited power."

The spotlight clicked off. He stood perched on the ledge of the orchestra pit not fifteen feet from me. A wide grin split his face while his mismatched eyes glared with his evil intent. He looked human enough, except for his one clear, blue eye and one solid, black eye and a distinct grey pallor to his skin. The Seeker had that grey look too. Apparently, centuries spent in the Underworld wreaked havoc on the complexion. Deep auburn hair hung to Barnabus' shoulders, where it brushed against his coal black cloak. He was clad head to toe in black, just as the Seeker had been. My inner smart aleck wondered if the all-black wardrobe was a necessity to remind themselves they were evil. Like if a member of the Dark Army accidentally threw on a powder blue polo shirt, they would get confused and book a tee time instead of trying to take over the world. If I wasn't terrified I was going to die, I may've asked.

"I have waited for you a long time. Longed for you. Finally, our time has come." In a grossly intimate way, he devoured me with his eyes. Relief flooded me at the unexpected ruckus from stage-left that broke his gaze, until the cause of it added a mind-blowingly stressful obstacle to this situation.

"Wha's going on?" Alec asked as he stumbled onto the stage. Apparently my definition of "get Alec to safety" differed from Keni's.

What... did she just drop him out the backdoor?

My eyes flicked back and forth between him and Barnabus. A wide grin of glee spread across Barnabus' face as he reveled in my panic. "Who's that? Hey! You're the guy that hit me! Wha's your problem buddy?"

"Did you enjoy my choice of bait?" Barnabus asked merrily. "I had every intention of finding a nun, small child, or your basic good Samaritan to lure you here. Then I stumbled on to him. This gawky man-child that just reeked of your scent! It was too perfect to pass up. Please humor me, for I must know, is he special to you?"

I hadn't answered that for myself yet. The diabolical fiend sure as heck didn't get to know before I did. "Why?" I asked tartly. "Were you going to ask me out? Because I gotta say my standards are lax, but I draw the line at psycho crack-pot. Sorry."

Raw hatred mixed with disgust flickered across his face, which I tried not to take personally. Quickly, his look of mocking and condescension returned. "You have a sharp tongue, girl. I think I'd like to cut it out and eat it."

"Eeeew. Dude that's really gross," Kendall grimaced as she rounded the curtain. She had no physical injuries that I could see. No doubt her wings took care of that for her.

"You cannot protect her, you spiky-haired twit," Barnabus sputtered. "Your presence here is completely inconsequential. I have waited too long. I will retrieve my prize."

"Even so. This is where I belong." She hooked her arm through mine and graced him with an angelic smile. Her normal sweetness and innocence were absent from her eyes. In their place lay steel.

"Wha's he talking about? Wha's going on?" Alec wondered aloud.

I held up a hand to silence him and addressed the deadly villain across from me. "The Gryphon and all he protects will never be yours Barnabus. We'll see to that."

The corners of his lips curled up wickedly. "But it will. That creature…" he spat the word out as if it left a bad taste in his mouth, "is dense and way too easily fooled. The gossip and murmurings that led him to call on you in the first place were all my doing. I had my men spread the word that we had found a way to enter his precious Spirit Plane and were coming for him. It was all a lie. A lie that seeped its way back to him and motivated him to channel his powers through a mortal. Imbecile that he is, he did it. Now all I have to do is kill you. He'll be weakened, and we will enter his realm. My army and I will take him down. Then all the power he harnesses and protects will belong to me. It's almost too easy."

"If it's so easy, why did it take you three centuries to come up with it?" I asked with venom in my voice.

He laughed that fiendish cackle again. "It didn't take long to come up with the plan. The rest of the time I was busy learning a few tricks to aid the process along. Would you like to see one?"

Okay, little side note here. If a psychopathic killer asks if you want to see a trick, say no. That's the smart thing to do. I, on the other hand, responded, "Bring it."

CHAPTER 30

Barnabus' mismatched gaze locked on mine as he casually stepped off the brick ledge and disappeared into the orchestra pit. No sooner did he vanish from sight than the ground began to tremble under our feet.

Being from Michigan, an earthquake was a new, terrifying experience for me. Where I come from, the ground stays put—a wonderful trait I took for granted up until that very moment. We stumbled from side-to-side, struggling to keep our footing.

"What's happening? We don't have earthquakes in Tennessee!" Alec yelled.

"I'm pretty sure it had to do with the guy that just jumped down there, and there's more to come. Really bad stuff. Seriously, Alec, for the sake of self-preservation, you need to run!"

But Alec didn't get his chance to run. None of us did. The shimmying ground came to a halt. Gabe stalked out from behind the curtain and stood protectively beside me.

"Whoa!" Alec yelped. He scampered away from Gabe and practically climbed onto Kendall's back. "Lion! Lion! Big friggin' lion!"

"It's okay. He's with us." Kendall patted his hand.

"You guys have a pet lion? Seems that should have come up in conversation!" Without channeling it, I knew Alec's feelings were a heaping mess of pain, horror, and confusion. However, the low, ominous hiss that began reverberating up from the orchestra pit told me things were about to get boatloads worse.

"Here we go," I prepped my team. Kendall's wings sprang to life and knocked her hanger-on to the ground. Gabe arched his back and let out an intimidating roar.

Legs splayed out before him, Alec murmured, "What the…"

The hiss became thunderous. Something unrecognizable began to rise up out of the pit. It was big—huge in fact. But I couldn't identify what the greenish-brown mound ascending toward the ceiling was.

Gradually the mass tipped in our direction. Two deep holes that dripped with ooze came eye level with us. Then it exhaled. My cohorts and I backpedaled frantically until our backs were pressed up against the back wall of the stage. We were staring down the snout of an enormous lizard. Thick scales covered its narrow, reptilian face. Its menacing, yellow-slitted eyes bore down at us. A forked tongue flicked out from between jagged, yardstick-sized teeth.

"That's a dragon! He turned into a dragon!" Kendall squealed and wrapped her wings around herself. "No one said anything about dragons! I don't do reptiles! And dragons just plain suck!"

As freaked out as I was, I really didn't want my shield to fly away. "Yeah, but as dragons go, he doesn't look that big!"

The dragon snorted out a malicious chuckle. Then, as if to deliberately prove me wrong, began to rise up out of the pit. Up and up and up until all we could see before us was a wall of rutted, deep olive scales. His head brushed the ceiling of the lofty theater as he towered over us. No denying it—he fit into the category of massively, undisputedly gigantic. Kendall was right. Dragons do suck.

The immense lizard swerved his lower body slightly. A long,

whip-like tail, complete with flesh-impaling spikes, swung at us. I grabbed the back of Alec's shirt and pulled him along as we dove to safety.

"He's pretty friggin' big, Cee!" Kendall snapped at me.

"Size doesn't mean anything! The bigger they are ..." My sentence got interrupted by the dragon belching flames at us. "... the larger the flames they spit! Kendall shield!"

Kendall leapt in front of us, her wings our umbrella of protection. I watched her face as the flames cascaded over her. She didn't seem to be in pain, but the exertion from the force of the erupting fire took its toll. I grabbed her upper arms to help support her. Her eyes met mine, but all she could manage was a brief nod.

Noticing that his wrath was being diverted, Barnabus stopped. Kendall didn't budge from where she was anchored, anticipating his next strike.

"Pretty birdie," Barnabus growled. His voice morphed into the satanic hiss Grams mentioned. With one jagged claw, he pointed at Kendall. He slowly raised his finger. At the same time, Kendall's feet left the ground. By her shocked, wide eyes, I knew this flight schedule had not been on her itinerary. Barnabus circled his extended digit, and Kendall spun around to face him. "Now move!" He demanded and flicked his finger. Kendall flew through the air, forcefully colliding with the wall. Had her wings hit first, she would've been fine, but she hit head first. I watched in dismay as she slid down into a heap on the floor.

"That's better," Barnabus hissed. In a swift, fluid motion, he ducked around us. His enormous body curled around the stage and blocked the exit. "You must be as dim as the Gryphon. It was so easy to lure you here. I just needed the right bait." His claws closed around a stunned Alec. "Hellooo, Bait!"

"No!" I screamed as his grasp tightened.

"You never told me just how you feel about this boy," Barnabus said in his malicious purr. He stood to his full height, his captor in

195

tow. "Do you love him? A crush, perhaps? Or, maybe just a naughty lusting? What is it?"

I was speechless. My earlier sarcasm completely silenced by my panic and terror. It was my job—no, my calling—to stop this from happening. But my emotions had me petrified into immobility.

Barnabus' eyes twinkled with joyous evil. "What seems to be the matter child? Do you not yet know how deeply your feelings for him lie? Well, it is my experience that the saying is very much true." With his free hand Barnabus placed one dagger-like talon directly under Alec's chin. Alec whimpered. "You never know what you have until it's gone."

Alec let out a blood curdling scream as the gargantuan beast slowly and methodically dug its claw into his tender flesh. Blood rained down and pooled on the stage at my feet.

CHAPTER 31

My head swam. Alec's agonized screams were cut off as blood spewed out of his mouth and over his lips. The magnitude of the horrific events before me reduced me to a paralyzed lump. Thankfully, Gabe sprang into action. He soared through the air. Teeth bared. Claws readied. As our chestnut-maned lion latched on to Barnabus' hand, he became a ferocious blur, biting and slashing with vengeful vigor.

Barnabus let out a pained holler and dropped Alec, who fell to the ground with a sickening thud. He lay still. I hoped he passed out in mid-trauma and not that the rescue came too late. Barnabus turned his full attention to Gabe and tried to shake off the enraged cat. The sight of Alec's body lying there like a discarded toy made me snap to. I took advantage of the diversion and quickly hooked my arms under his armpits to drag him outside. I made a conscious effort not to look at the gaping hole in his head or the blood that covered him and left a trail behind us. Going with the superhero stereotype, I wasn't supposed to puke or pass out in the face of adversity. Right now those were both very strong possibilities.

Through the darkened backstage and out the exit into the cool, crisp night air we went. As soon as I got him outside, I checked for his pulse. I had to know for sure if my failure to act cost him his life. Scared to see if his face had been reduced to hamburger, I opted for his wrist. Even that was covered with warm stickiness from the blood that seeped everywhere. The drumming through his veins was weak but steady. He desperately needed medical attention or for Kendall to heal him. I would personally see to it that he got one, if not both of those things. Just as soon as I took care of the three-story reptile that desperately needed a butt kickin'. I sprinted back to rejoin the battle.

Back in the theater, Barnabus whipped his spiked tail across the stage at Gabe, fixated on impaling him. The lion's fur was visibly wet with sweat as he darted, leaped, crouched, or dived to avoid each lash.

"Hey, Lizard Breath!" I yelled. "Don't tire yourself out before you and I get a chance to dance!"

The head of the massive dragon swung toward me. "You're absolutely right. I should not be wasting my time on this flea-ridden pest."

The villainous dragon stomped at me. The floor vibrated under my feet. Gabe—my sentry—ran to position himself between Barnabus and me. That lethal tail swung again.

"Gabe! Look out!" I screamed.

He turned back to face our enemy, his timing truly tragic. A barb from Barnabus' tail caught him in the chest. The air left his lungs in a heaved gasp. Then he tumbled through the air, caught up in the momentum from the lashing. The defeated lion soared off the stage and shattered two rows of theater seats into kindling as he crashed.

"Would you look at that," Barnabus tsked, curling his tail up in front of his face. "I ripped off a spike when I slaughtered your meat sack of a brother. What an annoying travesty."

Barnabus' goading probably would've been more effective if I hadn't taken that moment to notice that Kendall was no longer lying where she collapsed. I didn't spot her, but I knew she was back in play.

Barnabus misread my silence as mourning and grinned wickedly. "I feel generous, so I'll give you a choice. I can kill you quickly and savagely or slowly and painfully. Which shall it be?"

I coated my voice with heavy despair in a performance that would've made Kendall proud. "You've slaughtered my entire family. Please, have mercy and make my death quick."

"So be it," he said with a satisfied smirk, then lunged.

His teeth, hungry for a taste, snapped as he neared. I stood firm. The ugly face of the dragon turned sideways; his mouth opened wide. He intended to snap me in two. Hot, rank breath assaulted my nose as his jaws encased me. A split second before he could chomp down, I jumped and wedged my arms and legs against the insides of his mouth. He tried to bite down, but I pushed back with all the force I could muster. My right hand and foot dug into the bumpy ridges of the roof of his mouth. A thick layer of gooey saliva squished between my fingers. Unfortunately, that was still the more pleasant side. My left hand and foot got the distinct displeasure of being mashed into his moist, wriggling, sandpaper tongue.

The life of a superhero. Glamorous, no?

I succeeded in catching Barnabus off guard. He spastically flung his head but couldn't dislodge me from his mouth. I was stuck like a rogue popcorn kernel. The initial surprise wore off, and he became eerily still. A low chuckle rumbled up from his throat, accompanied by the smell of sulfur. I gaped directly down the gullet of the beast. Red and orange flames tore up his throat. I was about to be charbroiled.

Hmmm...I really should've seen that coming.

No time to dwell on my lack of foresight, I anchored my right hand and left foot then shifted the opposite limbs. Now both my hands were on his upper jaw. With the temperature rising by the second I latched onto his razor-sharp teeth. Blood ran down my arms as my palms sliced open, but I held fast. As the scorching flames came rushing at me, I pushed off with the balls of my feet. The dragon's spongy tongue worked as my spring board to flip myself up and out of the way. I landed straddling his snout.

"Get off my nose you nit!" he bellowed as he shook his head.

"No can do, Barney!" As boldly as I declared it, this comment was nothing but empty bluffing. With no history as a bull rider I was completely unprepared for the bucking and rearing Barnabus unleashed. Needless to say, I didn't stay on the full eight seconds. I careened through the air, the wind whistling past me.

With ease I tucked and rolled to absorb the impact of the fall. I landed behind the stage curtain and scanned the area for some kind of weapon. The only potential prospect was an American flag hung on a thick pole in the corner.

"I hope this doesn't make me a bad American, but it's for the good of the people," I rationalized as I pulled the sturdy pole out of its resting place and snapped it in two over my leg. The bottom half splintered into a perfect makeshift spear.

From the direction of the stage came the ominous, rumbling voice, "Where did you go, girl? Did you finally come to your senses and run?"

My new weapon in hand, I marched back out onto the stage. "Don't bet on that happening!"

A quizzical expression played across Barnabus' face, and my own, as we both took stock of my self-deprecating comment. That moment was fleeting once my enemy noticed I was wielding a sharp stick. His lizard lips curled up into what resembled a smirk. "A stick? That is your weapon of choice? What do you plan to do with that? Pick my teeth?"

I tossed the wooden lance back and forth between my hands. "Actually I was thinking of ramming it through your heart. How's that sound?"

The dragon lowered its head to my level. I readied my stick for a possible strike. "Do you really think you could do it, child? Take a life? That is a huge burden to bear. I have to say." His reptilian eyes shifted to give me a paltry once over. "I just don't think you have it in you."

I glared up at him. "I really hate it when people underestimate me."

He hissed out a laugh then stood up to his full height. His massive head craned toward me as he spread his oddly-sized dino-arms wide. "By all means, go ahead. Prove that you are nothing but a lowly killer, just...like...me."

Any other person in that position may've taken a moment to consider what he had just said. The ramifications of the act. If it meant they were evil too. Blah, blah, blah. The only thing I considered was that the ancient, demonic being just gave me a free shot. I didn't hesitate. I leapt into the air and landed on his midsection. Bracing myself to his chest with my knees, I reared back and used both hands to plunge the spike into him. The pole splintered into thousands of tiny toothpicks in my hands, but failed to even scratch his thick hide.

Barnabus roared with laughter. "Did you really think I would make it I that easy for you?"

"I'm not going to lie, Barns. I was really hoping."

"And the vigor you attacked me with! That was impressive! You didn't even hesitate! You truly are a fighter. It is almost a pity I'm going to exterminate you."

That last comment made me very aware of my proximity to the enemy. I pushed off with my legs and flipped gracefully backward. The giant reptile caught me, mid-backflip, in his crusty, scaly hand.

"Don't run off pigeon," he purred in that disturbing growl. "I have big plans for us." His grip crushed as he squeezed me. I tried to push back against him to no avail. As the pressure of his grasp increased, my breath caught in my throat. A searing pain in my side signaled that my recently mended rib cracked again. Black spots danced before my eyes. My consciousness threatened to give.

"Now then," Barnabus said in a casual tone that goes along with being the squeezer and not the squeezee. "If you would like to plead for your life, now would be the time."

Leaning in eagerly to hear my words, he eased up on his grip to allow me to speak. The air rushed back into my lungs. I sucked it in like a deep sea diver emerging from the depths. When the daunting darkness retreated from my head, I peered directly into the enormous eye of the dragon. My voice still came out a wheeze when I attempted to declare valiantly, "You won't make it out of this theater alive."

Barnabus' alligator-like snout crinkled into a snarl. "What are you hoping will happen?" he sneered. "Do you think your muscle bound brother and feather-brained sister are going to swoop in and rescue you? Perhaps you'd like to see what they're up to?"

He swung his massive frame around, me in tow. With the flip of his wrist he turned me in the direction of auditorium. There were Gabe and Kendall, in the exact same spot Gabe fell. Kendall's wings wrapped protectively around the fading lion. She glowed with her healing warmth, but my brother's hacked open chest wasn't healing. An ever expanding puddle of blood surrounded him. Kendall trembled from the strain. Sweat coated her flesh and soaked through her shirt. Still she fought. If she wasn't ready to give up, neither was I. Barnabus wanted this image to destroy my resolve. Instead it strengthened it.

I craned my neck to look back at his ugly mug. "Like I said, you won't get out alive."

All the air rushed out of my lungs in a gut wrenching whoosh as he constricted me in his white-knuckled fist. "You infuriating little pest! You cannot comprehend when you've been beaten can you? This is it! This is the end of you! You can say whatever you want. It ends here!"

As he screamed, he shook me viciously. My head wobbled so hard it felt like it might snap off my neck. Soon his rants turned into nothing more than a ringing in my ears. One by one, my senses gave up. They retreated into the dark abyss and waited for me to join them there. I hung on by a thread. My insides were squeezed by the agonizing death grip squashing me. But that paled in comparison to the panicked fire in my lungs as I tried in vain to gasp in even a whisper of air. The black spots returned. They bonded together to form a black curtain that blocked out the world. This time I couldn't fight it. Everything went black.

CHAPTER 32

*W*ake up! Wake up! Do you hear me, young lady?"

A familiar voice in the darkness, but the sleep is comforting. It takes away the pain. Movement means searing pain. Sleep, sleep is good.

"Celeste Marie Garrett! You have to wake up! You have to fight!"

Daddy? Is that you? Am I dead?

"No, not yet. But if you give up, you will be. You have to fight, Celeste. Too much depends on you."

It's too hard. I'm not strong enough. I can't do it.

"Yes, you can! You have to! Now wake up Celeste!"

"Wake up, Celeste!" My father's voice gave way to Kendall's urgent screams.

I pried my eyes open. The dragon's rough palm still grasped me. Yet, something caused him to loosen his grip just enough that air could return to my lungs. Weak, dizzy and light-headed, I let my head loll back as I peered up at ole lizard face. His narrowed eyes glared down at the ground directly in front of us.

I followed his gaze and grinned weakly at what I saw. One

perturbed-looking lion and an angry look-alike angel were in fighting stance at the foot of the beast. Between his teeth Gabe held the very barb that Keni extracted from deep in his chest. If it was made of the same substance as Barnabus' skin, it should be able to penetrate his scaly shell. Judging by the smug look on Kendall's face and the nervous expression Barnabus wore, I wasn't the only one who made that conclusion.

"Killing the two of you is becoming a tedious task," the dragon rumbled.

"Then stop." Kendall shrugged. "'Cause we're not crazy about it either."

"Not a chance," he hissed. His enormous body folded in half toward them as flames blasted from his jaws.

This time Kendall was ready for it. She rocketed up to meet the attack. With one wing curled over her head, she used it as a battering ram against the geyser of fire. The flames bounced off her. My scaly prison was another matter. The ricocheting flames beat against the dragon's claws, which just so happened to be holding yours truly. If Kendall concocted this plan as a way to get Barnabus to release me, there was one crucial flaw—I was in the way. My skin blistered as it was scorched. It prickled in excruciating pain. My nose and throat burned. My lungs ached from breathing in the smoke and flames. My eyes watered so badly that my vision blurred. A wall of red and orange blazed up around me. I was going to die before this overgrown gecko even got uncomfortable enough to let go. Clawing and squirming became pointless. I couldn't escape. I tried to scream for Kendall to stop but could only manage a hacking cough.

I am so glad I woke up for this. Would've been a pity to miss out on this whole burning alive experience.

For the first time all day, luck turned in our favor. The dragon screamed in agony and lost his hold on me. Our evil nemesis waved his hand frantically, blowing on it and screeching in pain.

I plummeted in a free fall, screaming my fool head off as the ground rushed up to meet me. My descent was short lived. Kendall swooped in and snagged me under the arms.

"You jumped off a building and landed without a scratch. What's with the drama?" she asked calmly.

"Habit." Without asking, I plucked one of her magical feathers.

"Ow!"

"Sorry, but after torching me up there you had that coming." I rubbed the feather all over me. This was faster than waiting for my rapid healing to kick in. The results were instantaneous, leaving no visible signs I had ever been grilled to a perfect medium-well.

"Feel better?" Keni asked.

"Much, thank you. Now if you could kindly drop me off on the chest of the horrible, hell-spawned beastie, I'd like to kill him so I can go home and take a bubble bath."

"No problem," my pilot said. "Next stop, hell beastie."

As she looped around the theater, making a wide arc back toward Barnabus, I sought out my weapon. "Gabe! Throw me the spike!"

Our cruising speed was a rapid one. We quickly closed in on our target. Yet Gabe hesitated. He eyed the dragon, then me, and back again.

"Gabe! Throw it to me!" Despite my screams, he seemed undecided. We were almost to the point of no return. The moment to act was at hand—and my hands were still empty.

"Gabe, get your big, furry head out of your butt and throw me the friggin' spike!"

The bulky cat heaved a deep, resigned sigh. With a flip of his head, he tossed the spike through the air and into my eagerly waiting grasp. I weighed it between my hands and turned it over to find the most comfortable, functional way to grip it.

We were close enough to see the light reflect off his swamp green scales when Barnabus regrouped. He spun toward us, flames tearing from his throat.

Kendall looped us under the flames and skimmed up the dragon's belly. "I believe this is your stop," she said and released me. I grabbed on to his midsection with my arms and legs in a koala bear grasp. Quick as I could, I shimmied upward to my target. "I'll try to distract him," Kendall yelled as she flew off. The trail of the flames followed her.

I was almost to my destination when the dragon screeched. His body lumbered this way and that, almost causing me to lose my grip. I glanced down. Gabe had latched onto the dragon's leg. He savagely scratched and bit into the scaly flesh. For a brief moment the lion lifted his mahogany head.

"*Go!*" he yelled remarkably clear for a feline.

"Gone!" I shouted back. I fought to hold on and wriggled my way up Barnabus' abdomen. Directly above the thumping heart of the beast, I stopped. Anchoring myself with my legs, I grasped the spike in both hands.

The sensitive region I was positioned in didn't escape Barnabus' notice. His sharp talons flew at me, ripping layers of skin off my back as he tried to knock me away. Had his energies been more focused he would've succeeded, but Gabe and Kendall divided his attentions just enough.

I ignored the pain and arced the spike over my head. With every ounce of strength I had, I plunged it straight down. I felt it cut through the rock-hard exterior of the beast, then plunge right into his soft, gooey center. An eardrum-piercing scream erupted from the dragon. His back arched, and he dug at his chest with panicked swipes. I dove off him and away from his feverishly racking claws.

Landing smoothly, I backed away from the towering creature. Slaying the dragon would seem less heroic if I got caught under him when he fell. Gabe and Kendall were soon by my side. No one spoke as we focused on Barnabus.

His frantic clawing faded fast, as did he. As the life slipped out of him, his shape shifted. He shrank from the enormous, terrifying dragon back to the demented man that had sought out evil. Time finally got the chance to take its long awaited toll on him. All the centuries that had bypassed Barnabus came rushing back to him. He aged right before our eyes. His skin, muscle, and bone melted away until a pile of dust was all that remained of the deranged, mad man.

"I really wish I had closed my eyes for that," Kendall squeaked.

"Uh-huh," I agreed.

Even Gabe nodded.

We stood in silence for a moment. It was over. Really over. We actually did it. We exchanged wide-eyed looks of amazement.

"Holy crap! We did it!" I marveled as I reached back to tighten my loose ponytail.

"And only two out of the three of us nearly died," added Kendall, the lucky one-third.

"We should probably work on those stats for next time."

"Absolutely."

Not all loose ends had been tied up yet, though. "Keni, Alec is outside. He's hurt bad. The bottom of his face is...well, it's pretty much gone. Could you go heal him? Then we'll take him to the hospital to have him checked out."

"I'll heal him, but no way am I looking at his missing face. Ick." She crinkled her nose as she turned to jog outside.

Gabe still eyed the space Barnabus occupied only moments ago. "Good to see you up and around. How'd that barb to the chest feel?"

He snorted and rolled his eyes.

"Seriously, that was scary stuff. You okay?"

His furry brow creased as he contemplated the dust pile. Had Kendall not regained consciousness when she did, he would be dead and he knew it. This was exactly the kind of deep emotional stuff my brother didn't handle well. I decided to be nice and spare him.

"You know, it's actually a really good thing you were in lion form when all this went down. Regular Gabe would've screamed like a little girl at the first sight of the dragon."

The lion's face pulled back in a grin as he swiped at me with his gigantic paw. It glanced off my shoulder and sent me stumbling forward. "Ow."

His smile widened.

"You should head back to the truck and change just in case Alec wakes up after she heals him," I suggested.

Gabe snorted his agreement then trotted off, his paws padding against the wood floor.

Left alone, I peered around the sprawling theater. The pile of dust, assorted scorch marks, broken flag pole, and rows of demolished chairs were the only remaining signs of what transpired here. To the outside world, it would look like nothing more than vandalism. No one would know it was where we had fought and prevailed over the forces of evil.

For now.

Somewhere out there, the Dark Army still longed for my head on a stick. A chill ran down my spine. I made a none-too-hasty retreat from the empty theater.

EPILOGUE

After spending a ridiculous amount of time primping and preening, I bounded down the stairs in Kendall's daisy-covered sundress. Even this early in the day, the house buzzed with activity. That was commonplace as of late. And with the bubbly, excited mood I was in, I welcomed it.

In the newly renovated living room, Kendall and Keith snuggled on the brand new glass-free leather sectional. Kendall had gone against our better judgment and told Keith everything. I mean everything. For the most part, he took it well. He was understanding and compassionate toward Keni, respectful and inquisitive around Gabe, and downright weirded out by me. Knowing I was some special "chosen one" freaked him out. I didn't think it was possible, but he got even more nervous and fidgety whenever I was around. The way he broke out in a visible sweat at the sight of me made me wonder if he thought I was going to flip out and rip his head right off his shoulders.

Silly boy, I would never do that. If for no other reason than it would tick Kendall off royally.

But the two of them were inseparable now, so I came to terms with the spastic, jittery kid. The sickeningly-sweet twosome were cuddled up watching Grams' new flat screen when I walked in. Kendall looked up and flashed me her winning smile. Keith immediately shifted his gaze to stare intently at a spot on the floor.

"Wow! Look at you! So today's the big day, huh?" Keni said.

"Yep." I nodded and spun so she could check out my entire ensemble.

"What ... what big day?" Keith asked daring to glance up at me briefly with nervous eyes.

"Celeste is going to go get herself a boyfriend today." Kendall's smile held the teasing tone reserved for sisters and best friends.

"Where?" Noticeable sweat soaked through his shirt.

"The grocery store," I deadpanned. "They keep them in the meat department right next to the tenderloin."

"Wait ... what?"

Kendall glared at me before turning to the aid of her anxious, sweaty sweetie. "She's making fun of you, babe. She's going to go see Alec."

"Aren't you afraid he'll freak out at the sight of you?" Keith blurted. His eyes popped open as big as saucers when he realized he may have just angered me. I stifled a laugh.

"Not a problem! She sent Gabe to scope things out for her," Kendall answered, oblivious to her boyfriend's agitation. "Alec couldn't remember a thing. So Gabe told him that he had been mugged and we, like, found him and rescued him while we were touring the campus with Cee."

"Now I have the all clear to ask him out without him screaming and running away," I quipped.

Kendall laughed. Keith winced.

"Even with Alec around, my boyfriend will still be the best, most perfect wubikins there is!" Kendall gushed, then pounced on a clearly uncomfortable Keith for a rather one-sided, incredibly awkward PDA.

211

Okay, I slay hell beasts, but that gave me the shivers. I bolted for the kitchen before I tossed my cookies on Grams' newly purchased zebra print rug.

In the dining room, Gabe searched for room on the table for his breakfast around the mess of books Grams had strewn everywhere. After she was released from the hospital, Grams demanded to know the entire story. Once we filled her in, she insisted we introduce her to our guide to all things supernatural. Upon their first meeting, I expected some sort of blow up. I was just waiting for Grams to spout off about Alaina filling our heads with nonsense. Her encounter with Barnabus must've impacted her enough that she listened to the whole tale intently. She absorbed everything enthusiastically. She even let Kendall heal her broken bones. After that, Grams became so passionate about our calling, she was ready to march in a superhero pride parade. Come to think of it, that would be a lonely parade. It would just be one crazy old lady in a leopard print bikini waving a banner.

"Ooh! Look at this one! It says there is a place on a person's hand that if you squeeze just right, you can render them immobile! That's a good one! She could use that!"

"Does it only work on humans?" Gabe asked between heaping mouthfuls of cereal. "'Cause it's not likely we'll be fighting people."

"I don't know. These books are really lacking in demonic stuff." Grams perked up when she noticed I entered the room. "Good, you're here! Which sounds more interesting, Judo or Jiu Jitsu?" In each hand she held up a dummies guide to both of the fighting methods.

"Nope. Not today, Grams. Today I'm just a normal girl."

"Normal is boring." She brushed off my statement and began flipping through the pages of one of the books. "This one has pictures. I could practice with you. It'd be fun."

Well, that idea is beyond terrifying. "Seriously, Grams. I'm not talking about anything superhero-ish today," I said, carefully dancing around the landmine she just laid out before me. "Today I am just Celeste."

"You're no fun, Celeste. How about you, Gabe? You want to learn martial arts with your grandma?" She turned her attention to my brother who was devouring his breakfast.

"Sure, why not? What guy doesn't want to watch his grandma break a hip?"

"I'm not going to break anything! And even if I did, it'd give me an excuse to go see Dr. Allyn again. Yummy!" She smacked her lips at that idea then buried her nose back in the book.

Gabe and I exchanged disgusted looks. That's when I noticed his breakfast. Before him was Grams' punch bowl filled with cereal.

"Geez, Gabe! Is there any cereal left?"

"Nope."

"I bought that box yesterday!" Grams stated.

"What? It takes a lot of energy to morph into a lion. Don't judge me."

"Not judging." I opened the cereal box and gazed in. Not a flake or a raisin left. "Just hungry!"

"Oh. Can't help you there. And PS—I ate all the bacon, too."

"Are you sure you don't turn into a pig instead of a lion?" I snapped.

"If he turned into a pig that would make him eating the bacon cannibalistic and gross," jabbed Grams.

My mouth fell open, stumped once again by her quick wit.

"All right, Grams! You rendered her speechless! I didn't think that was possible!" Gabe cheered and high-fived her over the table.

"Whatever. I'll grab something while I'm out." I grabbed my keys off the counter and shouldered my bag.

"Hey, wait. Can I come? I need to swing by the community college to get registered." Recent events had finally helped Gabe find a direction in life. He enjoyed coaching so much he decided to go back to school to become a teacher. While I was insanely proud of him, I really didn't want company today.

"How about tomorrow? I'm going up to the hospital to see Alec."

Gabe adopted an over exaggerated pout, lower lip out and the whole bit. "That's okay if you want to impede upon my academic achievement."

Unlike me, Grams fell for his act. She gave him a sympathetic look then shot me the stink eye.

"Oh, for crying out loud! Fine!" I relented. "But you're waiting in the car at the hospital!"

"Will you at least crack a window?" He smirked.

"Only if you promise not to eat my upholstery," I shot back.

"Then we should probably stop for snacks on the way."

There should be a support group for girls with obnoxious brothers.

Demons are predictable. You know they're going to try to kill you, and they don't disappoint. In the heat of battle, they aren't going to stop and say, "You know, this just isn't working out. It's not you...it's me. I just think I'd like to try to kill other people. Maybe we can just be friends?"

I wiped my sweaty palms on the sides of my dress and tried to calm my queasy stomach with a few deep breaths as I trudged down the hospital corridor to Alec's room. For a minute, I actually wished for a surprise demon attack because it seemed easier than telling a boy I liked him. How twisted is that logic?

Way too quickly I reached his door. Room 1192. I desperately hoped it would not be known henceforth as the final resting place of my last shred of dignity. Realizing there was no way to brace myself for what was to come, I swallowed my trepidation and pushed open the door.

As soon as I saw him, peacefully snoring away, my apprehension eased. I took a step forward. My head cocked to the side to admire him. Against the stark white sheets his strawberry-blonde hair looked almost auburn. His skin seemed paler than before, but not in a sickly way. It reminded me of the petals of a white rose—soft, silky, and inviting to the touch. Unable to curb the urge, I approached his bed and softly brushed the back of my hand against his cheek. He responded with a low moan. His head turned in my direction as his eyes fluttered open. Under the fluorescent lights in the room, they looked darker—a deep sapphire blue.

"Celeste?" Once his sleepy gaze focused, he grinned up at me.

I returned his smile, thrilled to see him awake and alive. "Hey. How ya feeling?"

He extended his hand, and I took it without hesitation. His skin was so warm, I wondered if he had a fever. "Better. My head's still a little fuzzy. But I'm getting stronger every day."

"Great. That's really just … great." My cheeks ached from the broad grin I was sporting.

Quicker than I could really comprehend, his grogginess vanished. He peered up at me with a focused intensity that made the butterflies in my stomach *Riverdance*. "I'm really glad you stopped by. I've been wanting to talk to you."

"Really?" I tried my best to sound nonchalant, but the rapid successions of my heartbeat left me breathless. I hoped I sounded Marilyn Monroe-esque and not like he should hit the call button and get me medical attention. "I had something I wanted to talk to you about, too."

"Mind if I go first?" he asked with a lazy smirk.

"Shoot."

He released my hand to use the push button to raise the head of his bed. Once he was re-adjusted, he leaned in and beckoned me closer with the curl of his index finger. My heart pounded in my chest as I happily obliged. The warmth of his breath on my face caused a heat to rise within me. I wanted more than anything to eliminate those last few inches between us and taste his sweet lips, but I restrained myself. Instead I focused on the sensual curve of his mouth as it parted to begin what I hoped would be the proclamation of his feelings for me.

"Celeste?" My name came out a throaty moan. Chills danced across my skin.

"Yes?"

"Who was the man that turned into the dragon?"

I snapped back as if he'd slapped me. "What?"

My shocked reaction seemed to amuse him. "Now, now. Don't play dumb. You know exactly what I'm talking about."

My mouth fell open. As someone that knows firsthand what a punch to the gut feels like, I can say that this took my breath away in the same fashion. Words failed me. I opened and closed my mouth hoping some brilliant explanation would tumble out, but all I could muster was, "I ... I have no idea what you're talking about."

Alec lowered his chin. Condescension dripped from his expression. "Really? That's how you're going to play this? You're gonna feign ignorance? How original."

"I'm not feigning anything." My voice lacked any conviction.

He casually raked a hand through his hair, causing the locks to stick up off his head in messy spikes. My brows drew in. I thought it was the lighting, but now I wasn't so sure. Had his hair actually changed color?

"I guess I must have imagined the red-haired guy that shifted into a dragon and meat-hooked my face with his talon .... while you just stood there and watched ... not lifting a finger to help me."

"Maybe it was a dream," I muttered, grasping for anything to get me out of this.

He licked his lips and looked me up and down hungrily. "If it was a dream, you would've been wearing a lot less, and calling me Master."

"Alec!" I snapped, appalled he would say such a thing.

Like someone talking in their sleep, my harsh tone seemed to wake him. He jerked and blinked rapidly. When he looked my way again the darkness had vanished from his eyes, in its place was fear and confusion. "Celeste? What ... what happened? When did you get here?"

"Just now." My eyes narrowed. "You don't remember?"

He bit his lip and shook his head. Frustration creased his brow.

"No. I'm sorry. Ever since I hit my head, I keep having these— episodes. I just kind of blackout. The doctor says it has to do with my concussion. It should correct itself with time. Whatever the reason, I hope they go away quick. They're scary as all hell." He paused as he took in my tense body language, then his shoulders sagged. "You look freaked. Did I say something bad?"

I forced on my most reassuring smile, despite my utter confusion. For a brief moment Alec had seemed—demonic. Was that really remnants of a concussion or something much, much worse?

"No," I lied. "It wasn't bad."

He expelled a sigh of relief as his head fell back against his pillow. "Good. I'd hate it if I said or did anything that hurt you." His hand found mind and he gave it a squeeze.

"I know that." Without the bother of a segue I asked, "So, what happened to you? Do you remember?" I traced my thumb over the tops of his fingers, all the way internally praying his answer wouldn't involve anything scaly.

"Nope, not a thing. Just remember waking up here getting a sponge bath from a very man-ish female nurse."

That transitioned my smile from fake to genuine. Whatever had happened a moment ago had passed. He was my Alec again.

"I'm glad you came," he murmured. "I've missed you." Gently he gave my hand a tug and pulled me to him. I didn't hesitate. I perched on the edge of his bed and twined my arms around his neck. My head nestled on his shoulder. A snap from his hospital gown pressed into my cheek, but I didn't care. I just wanted him to hold me.

Alec nuzzled into my hair and inhaled deeply. He groaned as if I smelled intoxicating. "Your smell isn't even human." His voice came out a low rumble. "What are you?"

I ripped myself away from him and stared into glowering eyes the color of midnight. One dramatic leap and my back was up against the door, the knob digging into my spine. "Alec?" I reached behind me and fumbled for the door knob.

Again his face cleared. He shook his head and rubbed his temples as if these flashes were causing him pain. "It happened again, didn't it? I'm so sorry. They don't usually happen that close together. I don't know what's going on."

Neither did I. More than I had ever wanted anything in my whole life, I wanted this to be a medical condition easily remedied. But if it wasn't, if what I feared was true ... No. I couldn't even think it. This was Alec. I could never hurt him. And yet, I already had. The only reason he was lying in that bed in the first place was because of me. Whatever was happening to him, it was my fault.

My hand secured around the knob, and I yanked the door open. "I'm sorry Alec. About everything. But, I have to go." Because if I stay, I may have to kill you.

"Celeste, please wait." The desperation in his voice was enough to make me glance back. Pain gripped my heart at the tears that had welled in his—once again—crystal blue eyes. Anguish etched his face. He looked so lost. So confused. "Please don't go. I'm scared. I...I don't understand what's happening to me."

I paused. Indecision tugged me relentlessly in both directions. I closed my eyes and took a step. The door banged shut behind me.

THE GRYPHON SERIES CONTINUES WITH *EMBRACE*,
AVAILABLE NOW!

About the Author

Stacey Rourke is the award winning author of works that span genres, but possess the same flare for action and snarky humor. She lives in Michigan with her husband, two beautiful daughters, and two giant dogs. Stacey loves to travel, has an unhealthy shoe addiction, and considers herself blessed to make a career out of talking to the imaginary people that live in her head.

Visit her at www.staceyrourke.com
Facebook at www.facebook.com/staceyrourkeauthor
or on Twitter or instagram @Rourkewrites.

If you enjoyed The Conduit, pick up these other titles by Stacey Rourke:

THE GRYPHON SERIES
Embrace
Sacrifice
Ascension
Descent
Inferno
Revelation

The Legends Saga
Crane
Raven
Steam

Reel Romance
Adapted for Film
Turn Tables

UNFORTUNATE SOUL CHRONICLES
Rise of the Sea Witch
Entombed in Glass

TS901 Chronicles
Co-written with Tish Thawer
TS901: Anomaly
Coming Soon: TS901: Dominion

Veiled Series
Veiled
Coming Soon: Vlad

www.ingramcontent.com/pod-product-compliance
Lightning Source LLC
Chambersburg PA
CBHW051434170626
46809CB00006B/2455